REBEL

REBEL

Willo Davis Roberts

SCHOLASTIC INC.

New York Toronto London Auckland Sydney
Mexico City New Delhi Hong Kong Buenos Aires

ISBN 0-439-68614-8

12 11 10 9 8 7 6 5 4 3 2 1   4 5 6 7 8 9/0

Printed in the U.S.A.   40

First Scholastic printing, September 2004
Book design by O'Lanso Gabbidon
The text of this book is set in Janson.

*To the kids and grandkids and great-grandkids—
past, present, and future—
with thanks for their inadvertent
contributions to my books.*

Her name was Amanda Jane Keeling, but from the time she was two years old, everybody called her Rebel.

At the age of ten months her first word was "No." Her speech progressed to "No!" and "NO!" and finally to *"NO!!"* at full shriek before her parents were able to begin to moderate her verbal resistance.

She resisted strained spinach. She resisted potty training and help in fastening the buckles on her shoes, insisting, "Me do it," wanting no instruction or assistance from anyone else. She demanded her own choice in clothing, insisting on overalls and jeans from an early age, though she did eventually give in to dresses for Sunday school and her grandmother Clara's birthday parties. Gram Keeling couldn't have cared less what was worn to *her* parties.

At barely age five Rebel resisted the conformity of kindergarten. She behaved badly enough so that the teacher suggested perhaps they should hold her out of school until she was six and see if that didn't make a difference.

Nobody could figure out why she refused to be a kindergartner. With parents and three older brothers coaching her, she already knew how to read and write on a simple level; she was adept with crayons and poster paints, and she was not antisocial or painfully shy. Among the neighborhood children in her own age group, she was invariably the leader. She made up stories and instructed the other kids in how to act them out. Rebel, of course, designed the sets and the costumes, even at five. She was also often the heroine in the most flamboyant cloak and gown.

She had no objection to going to Sunday school; that was a firmly established family custom, and she excelled at her papers and craft work. "It's not that much different from kindergarten," Iris Keeling said of her daughter, "so why is she being so obstinate? If she's this bad at five, what is she going to be like when she hits puberty?"

"Heaven only knows," Grandma Clara said with a sigh.

"She'll probably outgrow it before that," Gram Keeling said. "Or maybe she'll turn out like me and be a rebel all her life."

Inwardly Iris shuddered at the thought and determined to try harder to make a compliant little lady out of her only daughter.

The entire family trembled in expectation of the resistance they would meet when it was mandatory to

WILLO DAVIS ROBERTS

send Rebel to school at six. She, however, picked out her new clothes—a plaid skirt, a white blouse, and a red sweater with matching knee socks—and was up the opening morning before anyone called her. Her auburn hair was combed, though not neatly parted, and she announced that since it would be a long day, she'd like toast with her cereal that morning.

"There'll be a snack time, I think," Iris said, unnerved by this apparent unprecedented change of attitude.

"I'll have the toast anyway, just in case," Rebel said.

And she adjusted to kindergarten as if she'd been born to it. It was a surprise to everyone but Rebel when six weeks into the school year, they promoted her to the first grade, where she was quite at home and immediately became a leader there as well as in her own backyard.

She had learned some discretion now, over her fourteen years, but she still had a tendency to discount other people's opinions and warnings. She needed to prove a thing for herself before she was satisfied, and that often meant taking a risk.

She had a few scars from some of the earlier risk takings.

There was still a small burn scar from the time she learned that "hot" really meant a stove was not to be touched. She currently had a black toenail from having dropped a rock on it after her brother Wally had expressed his opinion that it was too heavy for her to lift. She had an abraded area on one hip where she'd taken a curve biking on a gravel road and gone into a slide. When her mother gazed at the resulting damage with the comment that it was the second such mishap in a little over a month, Rebel had dismissed the injury. "It'll heal," she said.

"But the pants won't. This is the second pair, Rebel. At least stick to jeans that are already worn out when you do that kind of thing."

"Whatever," Rebel said agreeably.

The scar under her chin, where she had had ten stitches after jumping off the side of a diving board instead of diving off the end into deeper water, hardly showed now unless she tipped her head way back. And the arm broken when she fell out of a tree while tussling with Wally over a favorite teddy bear—she in the tree, Wally tugging from the ground—had long since healed without visible evidence.

"Why didn't you simply let go of the teddy bear when you felt yourself being pulled off the limb?" Iris had asked.

And Rebel made her usual commonsense reply: "Because it was *my* bear."

She had come downstairs on the last Saturday morning before school was out to hear multiple voices in the kitchen. *Gram!* she thought. *Gram is here!*

She had obviously brought fresh doughnuts and pastries, because the aroma drifted up the stairs to meet Rebel. *No cold cereal today*, she thought happily. She hoped Gram had some kind of project to get involved in today, since her best friend, Rachel, had gone to visit a

WILLO DAVIS ROBERTS

sick aunt in Puyallup and Rebel was on her own.

She knew it was Gram who provided the doughnuts, because her mother, while not a fanatical health nut, never bought anything with that many nutritionless calories. Sure enough, there was an open box in the middle of the kitchen table, and the whole family was sitting or standing around with powdered sugar drifting down their fronts or licking maple cream off their fingers.

"Mom," Wes Keeling was saying as Rebel reached over her father's shoulder for a jelly doughnut, "that's the craziest thing you've come up with yet."

"Why?" Gram asked complacently. She added a packet of creamer to her coffee and reached out an arm to snake it around Rebel's middle, smiling up at her. "You know, Wes, you wonder how Rebel here got to be the way she is, and all you have to do is look at yourself. You have rebelled against anything I ever tried to do—or get you to do—from the day you were born."

"Mother, you're sixty-four years old. It's time you settled down to something less difficult and risky."

"That's what you told me when I tried raising beagles. I enjoyed it thoroughly, and I got Pookie out of it, didn't I? Couldn't have a more satisfactory companion than Pookie."

At her feet the small beagle heard his name and thumped his tail, then nudged his mistress for the expected treat.

While Gram approved of doughnuts for people, she carried a pocketful of miniature dog treats for Pookie, and she obediently produced one for him, smiling indulgently.

"Oh, and that was a smashing success, wasn't it? Raising dogs?" There was a perceptible trace of sarcasm in Wes's tone.

"A thing doesn't have to be a financial success to be satisfying," Gram informed her older son. "An old lady is entitled to do some things just for the fun of it."

Wes, who resembled his mother strongly except for the fact that his hair was still black while hers had gone softly white, leaned back in his chair. "Why is it that you're only a helpless old lady when you want sympathy and support, and the rest of the time you're young enough to tackle wild broncs?"

Rebel bit into her doughnut as she withdrew, hoping her father wouldn't notice that a tiny bit of raspberry jelly had dripped onto the back of his shirt. Surreptitiously, she swiped at it with a paper napkin and then wiped her mouth as if that were all she'd intended in the first place. Dad didn't seem to notice.

Mom was regarding her mother-in-law with the same expression she'd often directed at her daughter. "It seems rather extreme, Mother. At your age most people are thinking of . . . retiring, not starting a new business. And even giving up your nice apartment—"

"I'm tired of my nice apartment. I'm tired of assisted living among seniors who don't want to do anything interesting. There's a big need among college students for living quarters, and I just love this big old house—"

WILLO DAVIS ROBERTS

"A big old house is just what you don't need to take care of—"

"They'll all take care of their own rooms. And I'll get one of them to vacuum the public rooms periodically, give him or her a discount on the rent. Rebel, that thing is leaking filling down your arm."

Rebel caught it with her tongue, relishing its texture and flavor. Mom's idea of snacks was fruit, which was okay, but not delicious.

"What're you up to, Gram? Buying a boardinghouse?"

"No, a rooming house. There's a difference. I don't want to cook for anybody; they can have kitchen privileges or microwaves or hot plates in their rooms. I'm going to be partners with my friend Viola. She's had it with assisted living too."

"Mother, we're simply concerned for your welfare. You've worked hard all your life—"

"And I've got a few good years left, for Pete's sake. I don't want to spend them twiddling my thumbs. You're a good boy, Wesley, but you've never been sixty-four and bored. I'm bribing you all with goodies to keep you in one spot long enough to find out what you're going to be doing with your summer. I need a little almost-free labor, fixing up this place. Painting, a little wallpapering, odds and ends. Doing the stuff on ladders that we two old ladies"—and here Gram smiled sweetly—"don't want to climb. So what's on the agenda?"

After the small silence—surely they had told her?—all three of the boys spoke at once.

"We're competing in the music festival in Salzburg in June," James and Conrad said together.

"We're all going to Europe," Wally added. It was clear from his face that he had no interest in painting or repairing an old house, even for Gram.

"What about you, punkin?" Gram asked, turning to Rebel where she'd sunk onto a chair and was wondering if she could get away with a second pastry without eliciting a reprimand. "You going to the music festival too? Or could you be persuaded to help your poor old grandma in a new venture? Viola's grandson is going to be joining us. He's about your age, I think."

Having met Viola a time or two, and finding her to be a bit eccentric, Rebel wasn't exactly thrilled at the expectations for the grandson. Still, she was less than enthusiastic about spending several weeks at a music festival attended largely by people who spoke languages other than English, and listening to the same violin, cello, and flute parts she'd been hearing practiced at home for months.

She licked jam off her fingers and reached for the white pasteboard box. There was one maple bar left and her mother wasn't looking at her, so she took it as unobtrusively as she could with so many people sitting around the table; if she got a bite out of it, they probably wouldn't take it away from her. She chewed and swallowed the first mouthful before she spoke. "I kind of hate to miss the European tour that's planned after the festival. Dad's got a caravan rented— that's a small motorhome—and we're supposed to drive through Germany and Austria and Switzerland for a couple of weeks. Maybe I could stay behind and help you until it's time to do that, and fly over and join everybody else the end of the month."

"Well, even a couple of weeks of help would be something," Gram said. "How about it, folks? She's old enough to travel on her own. I'll put her on a plane at Sea-Tac and it'll be nonstop to wherever you decide to pick her up in Germany."

"Oh, Rebel!" Mom said, disappointed. "We've been planning and saving for this for such a long time—"

"So how would it spoil anything if I missed the music festival part of it?" Rebel asked. There was a carton of orange juice sitting in front of her and she poured a glass and drank some of it. "I'd still be there for the fun part—caravanning around foreign countries with the rest of you before you came home." She would also, for the first time ever, be on her own—well, Gram would be with her, but she was so laid-back it would be almost the same as alone—without her entire family. There was an intriguing pull to this idea.

She could tell by their faces that neither of her parents was embracing this concept with open arms.

Gram suddenly laughed aloud. "You're thinking you don't want to leave your precious daughter with this flake of a grandmother. Well, I'm no more of a flake now than I've been all my life, and I managed to raise you and both your brothers so you turned out all right, didn't I?"

Wes looked at her rather grimly. "You made it uphill work sometimes, Ma."

"The challenge was good for you. Look at you now, a successful educator. Summers off so you can take your family on a trip to Europe. Give me credit for instilling in you a good set of values—the Golden Rule—and a work ethic that's the equal of the best in the country. I may not always have been around to fix your meals, and you had to shift for yourselves more than any of us liked, but you learned to be independent at an early age. The experience will be good for Rebel. Give her a chance to find out what it's like to get out of the nest for a few weeks."

Rebel concentrated on finishing her maple bar before anyone noticed. She didn't care strongly one way or the other which she was allowed to do. But she wasn't especially interested in the music festival, and she did love Gram and enjoyed doing things with her. If Viola's grandson turned out to be a gigantic zero, it would only be for a couple of weeks.

Rebel felt no prickle of apprehension. She seldom did when she contemplated a new or different experience. After all, how could she know how things would turn out unless she tried them?

And that was how it began, that Rebel was launched into most eventful few weeks in her life so far. Because they eventually decided that it wasn't likely any harm would come from her staying behind to help Gram, though if they'd had a crystal ball their response might have been quite different.

2

Naturally Mom started to have second thoughts the minute Gram was out of earshot.

"Rebel's never been away from us before," she said. "I'm not sure she's ready for that."

There were lots of things Rebel had never done before, but she didn't intend to let that stop her trying all kinds of things. "Mom! I'm fourteen! That's practically grown-up. What could happen to me that wouldn't if you were still here at home?"

"I don't know," her mother said thoughtfully, "but knowing you, there's likely to be something."

"If you're remembering the time I scoured the neighborhood for pop cans and took off on my own with the proceeds to see a movie, remember I was only four. That was a long time ago."

"I was thinking of the time the school bus driver forgot to get an accurate head count the day you decided to stay at the zoo overnight . . . in the herpetology exhibit." Involuntarily Mom shivered. She'd never liked snakes very much, even the harmless varieties. "We didn't know what had happened to you for *hours*. We thought you'd been kidnapped by some maniac."

Rebel refrained from reminding her that she had never been in any danger and all the panic had been completely unnecessary. True, the bus driver had been reprimanded, but she hadn't lost her job over the incident, so no real harm had been done. She still remembered with pleasure how much fun it had been to be alone with all those snakes and to be able to study them closely for hours.

"I was seven, Mom. A long time ago. I know better than to get into any such situation again because it upsets you." She refrained, as well, from stating the fact that none of the things she'd ever done had upset *her* the way they did her parents, and no real harm had ever come to her. "You don't have to worry about me anymore. I won't do anything stupid."

For a disconcerting moment or two, her mother studied her, evaluating this statement.

"Well, remember, Rebel," Iris said. "If you have any problems, call Uncle George to come and get you."

Her husband, who had remained silent during this exchange, ran a hand through his slightly thinning hair. "For Pete's sake, honey, if she's old enough to be left here with Ma, she's old enough to have that much sense, too. My mother's right; she raised me and George and Tom, and we all survived."

"I want her to do more than *survive*, Wes. I want her to be safe."

"So what's going to happen to me," Rebel said impatiently, "just staying in this new-old house Gram's bought? Don't worry. I'll be fine."

Mom meant well, but she was a bit of a fussbudget. Other people's moms, like her friend Rachel's, just let their teenagers make their own decisions, take their own responsibilities, and sometimes Rebel wished her own mother could simply relax a little bit.

The rest of the family wasn't leaving the United States for three more days, but Gram was ready to carry her off to the new project on Friday evening. That was what helped sell the move; Rebel could change her mind about staying any time during those three days. She was surprised that her mother didn't insist on following them into Seattle to the new-old house to inspect it in person, but she had too much packing—and too little suitcase space—to allow her the time, thank goodness.

Rebel wasn't especially excited about helping Gram. After all, it was going to be a lot of work, rather than relaxation and play. But she and Gram liked the same movies and books, and no doubt they'd veg out during the evenings and eat yummy stuff Mom never had in the house. And she'd been to music competitions before and been bored out of her skull.

It wasn't that she didn't enjoy music, though the kind that her brothers played was not exactly easy listening. She'd always wondered why, in a family of musical geniuses, she alone had been left out. She wasn't tone deaf, and she had a nice singing voice, but beyond that she had no musical talent whatever.

By the time he was three, her brother James was begging for violin lessons. His teacher had raved over his ability with such tiny fingers on his miniature instrument. Conrad took naturally to the cello. When Wally came along, his choice was woodwinds, and he'd tried several different ones before settling on the flute.

And then there was Rebel.

The family had waited expectantly for her to request lessons on the grand piano that Iris loved but had never had enough talent on it to become a professional. When Rebel first reached up and *plinked* a few keys experimentally, they all smiled. Rebel would be a pianist.

However, an attempt to sit her on the bench beside Mama and show her how it was done resulted only in disappointment. Rebel mutinously shook her head. *No.*

"Maybe when she's a little older," Iris said hopefully.

They tried again when she was three. When she was four. When she was five and a half. While she danced to the tunes played on television and sang along with the themes on her favorite shows, she had no inclination to play the piano.

"Rebel is being Rebel," Gram said, with an *I knew it ahead of time* tone of voice.

Rebel knew she was a terrible disappointment to her parents. Not only did she have no compulsion to make music, she was totally disinterested in the sporting events that kept the rest of the family mesmerized when they weren't practicing Mozart or Bach. She *appreciated* classical music, but enough was enough. Listening to the others did not spur her on to compete against her brothers or to join them.

There was also the matter of her height.

"What a pity," she'd heard Grandma Clara say when she thought Rebel was not listening. "It's hard for a girl to be six feet tall."

She *wasn't* six feet tall, her father's height. She was only five feet ten, but that was eight inches taller than her exquisitely proportioned mother and taller than her youngest brother, Wally, who was still growing. She hoped and prayed that she had stopped growing by now.

By sixth grade she was the tallest girl in her class, a good head taller than any of the boys.

"They haven't even begun their growth spurts yet," Dad told her. "Don't worry. Stand up tall and keep your spine straight. You're going to be a stunning young woman, and by the time you get out of high school there'll be plenty of guys taller than you are."

It wasn't much comfort now. She'd gotten used to the stupid comments—"How's the weather up there?" "How come you're not on the basketball team?" "Here's Goliath, and she's a girl! Have you met David yet?"

It was an effort to stand tall when she was in a group and towered over everybody else. Yet she'd recognized that she did look much more attractive when she didn't slump, so there she was, a full head taller than virtually everybody else.

Even her mother occasionally made a thoughtless remark. "It's so handy to have someone around who can reach things on the top shelf when Wes and James aren't home."

"Thanks, Mom. Just when I'd convinced myself that I was actually petite," Rebel said with an edge to her voice.

"I *am* petite, and I never found it to be an advantage particularly," Iris responded.

"Except when a boy looked at you and thought you were pretty. After you stood up, he was still interested," Rebel said, stinging after a recent episode at a school dance.

Still, now, she supposed her height would be an advantage helping Gram Keeling with her new-old house. She'd be able to reach much higher than Gram without having to climb a ladder.

She'd been in the University District before and was familiar with the big old-fashioned homes, some of them with signs out front indicating that they functioned as fraternity or sorority houses. She didn't know if her parents were correct in thinking Gram might have bitten off more than she could chew with a rooming house for college students, but Rebel couldn't see any reason why she shouldn't try anything she wanted to do. She certainly understood the reluctance to settle for assisted living among people who had few interests and didn't want to be any more active than thumbing their remote controls.

Gram picked her up in her eight-year-old Oldsmobile, pale lavender in color. "So I can find it in a parking lot when I've forgotten where I left it," Gram had announced with satisfaction when the boys commented on the color. "It's the only lavender one in sight, no matter where I am."

"Works for me," Wally said. "And the color guarantees that none of your grandsons will want to borrow it."

It ran well for the most part, and when it got balky, Gram wasn't above diving under the hood and tinkering. Rebel had tried to imagine her mother using a wrench or a screwdriver and utterly failed. If she was around when Gram played mechanic, it seemed to Rebel like a wise thing to watch and learn. Who knew how much grief she might be spared some day in keeping a vehicle of her own operating?

"You can't do much with newer cars, though," Gram had warned. "They deliberately make them so you have to pay a garage to fix them. Watch Pookie when we get there, will you? He wants to explore, and I mislaid his leash somewhere. Keep your eye out for it."

The house was one of many enormous, old-fashioned structures that lined a short street a couple of miles from the U-Dub, as the University of Washington was fondly called.

The Olds coughed a couple of times when Gram

turned off the ignition. "What do you think?" she asked, obviously expecting admiration.

"Big," Rebel acknowledged, bending her head to peer upward out the car window. "Old. It *does* have electricity and indoor plumbing, doesn't it?"

Gram gave her a scornful glance. "I'm old. I'm not senile."

"Nope. Never thought you were. Wait, Pookie, not yet. I'll carry you inside until we find your leash. I suppose I'm being appointed chief dog exerciser?"

The little beagle wagged his tail enthusiastically and licked at Rebel's chin when she picked him up from the backseat.

"Yep. There are plastic bags and gloves inside the top of the bag of dog food," Gram said, heading for the trunk to unload.

Plastic bags and gloves. I've also been appointed chief pooper-scooper, Rebel thought, resigned. Still, she really liked Pookie, the only survivor of Gram's ill-fated attempt to raise pedigreed dogs. And the laws said that if you were going to have dogs in the city, you had to clean up after them.

Rebel stood on the cracked and slanting sidewalk, which was raised up by the enormous trees poking through the concrete, and looked up at the house. Three full stories of Victorian splendor. Well, except that the paint maybe needed refurbishing. It was white with faint touches of lavender and deep purple on the gingerbread trim. She wondered if the color scheme had influenced Gram's decision to buy it.

A faint movement caught her eye and Rebel hesitated, watching a window overhead where she was sure the curtains had twitched. "Somebody's watching us," she observed. "Spooks, maybe. It looks like the sort of house that would have some. You don't have any renters yet, do you?"

"No. Viola's grandson is painting a sign to hang there on that wrought-iron post. We're not quite ready for anyone to move in yet. Vi's car isn't here, but maybe she left the boy."

Rebel didn't know whether to allow a stirring of hopeful interest to arise. Viola barely came up to Rebel's chin. What if her grandson was the same size? "How old is this kid?" she asked, snuggling Pookie against her chest as they went up the front steps.

"Fifteen or so, I think. Can you hold that screen door while I get the other door unlocked?"

"Has he hit his growth spurt yet?" Rebel wondered out loud as they made their way inside.

"Oh, I'd say he's in the middle of it," Gram responded, depositing the carton she was carrying on a hall table. "You can let Pookie run loose inside."

The house proved interesting on the inside as well. The rooms were spacious, with high ceilings that even Rebel wasn't going to be able to reach without a ladder. She lowered Pookie onto the hardwood floor—not in bad enough shape so they'd have to worry about refinishing them immediately, Gram noted—and immediately the little dog lifted a leg and made a puddle.

Rebel yelped and grabbed for him, but it was too late.

"Paper towels in the kitchen, back that way. Guess I kept him cooped up too long. If you can find his leash, take him outside for a minute. And he's probably hungry, too. I'll finish carrying in the rest of the boxes."

"I thought you were housebroken," Rebel scolded as the beagle followed her down a long hallway, past double parlors on one side and a huge dining room on the other.

"Not his fault," Gram called after them. "I should have taken him out sooner."

The kitchen, which Rebel found after she'd had passed the bottom of the stairs that rose to a landing before turning at a sharp angle to reach first the second floor and then the third, was in proportion to the rest of the house. Big, kind of chilly, with old-fashioned appliances and an enormous table in the center of the room.

Pookie frisked around her feet, yipping encouragingly.

"Do I feed you first or go wipe up the puddle? All right, food it is. Just sit, okay?"

Promptly the beagle plopped his behind on the linoleum, lifting his head expectantly.

Usually Gram bought very large bags of dog food. No obvious storage place presented itself, so Rebel crossed to what she hoped was a utility room.

"Aha! I wonder if she stuck your dishes in the top of the bag. All right, here they are, one for water and one for food. And here's the missing leash, too!"

Pookie was wagging his entire body by this time. Rebel knelt to clip the leash onto his collar, deciding that an immediate trip to the backyard might be a strategic move, when a rather deep voice interrupted her in mid-move.

"Excuse me, I think you're dipping into our dog food."

Rebel swiveled on her heel, eyes still at floor level, and encountered the biggest pair of shoes she'd ever seen.

Slowly she tipped her head, traveling up—and up and up some more.

Good grief! How tall is he?

While she crouched there, fingers automatically completing the job with Pookie's leash, neck developing a crick, he answered the question that had formed in her mind.

"Six feet six. The air up here is fine, I don't get nosebleeds from the altitude; no, I'm not a basketball player and don't aspire to be, and the Nikes are size sixteen. They have to be specially ordered."

Rebel rose slowly to her feet. Gigantic. Not a zero, though. She recognized by the flicker on his face that her own height surprised him. "Five ten," she announced, resisting the compulsion to announce her weight as well. "I'm Rebel Keeling. I assume you're Viola's grandson."

He hesitated. "Moses Adams."

She couldn't stop the way her eyebrows rose briefly.

"Moses? Like the one who parted the Red Sea so the fleeing Israelites could cross ahead of Pharaoh's army?"

"Would that I could live up to my namesake," Moses said flatly. "Given me by my maternal grand-mother, who was rather a strange lady. I command no magic, unfortunately. That *is* our dog food, isn't it? Old Vi said I should feed the dog." He cast a disparag-ing glance at Pookie. "That *is* a dog, right?"

"Yes, Pookie's a beagle. He's not full grown yet, but he's definitely a dog. And I'm afraid you're mistaken about the ownership of the dog food, but you're wel-come to borrow some. There's plenty."

He was a rather nice-looking boy, Rebel decided. Thick brown hair, brown eyes behind wire-rimmed glasses, a good strong nose and chin, teeth that might have had recent orthodontic assistance, so perfect were they.

"You sure about the dog food? Old Vi said she'd left a bag in here."

"This is the only one I've found so far, leaning against the washing machine. And it's definitely Pookie's because his dishes and leash were in the top of it." She scooped a dishful of the dry food and then stepped to the laundry tub to run the second bowl full of water. Pookie ate and drank as if he'd been deprived all day.

"Pookie?" Moses echoed. "What kind of name is that for a dog?"

"My grandma's idea. I'd have named him some

good ordinary male name like George. I think his pedigreed name is something like Alfred Lord Tennyson the Fifth, which is quite a mouthful for a puppy, so he's Pookie."

"Don't you feel embarrassed when you have to call him in public?"

"Don't know. Haven't done that yet, but probably yes," Rebel said. It made her feel rather peculiar to be standing before a boy only a little older than she was, an *attractive* boy, and not be looking at the top of his head. In fact she was close enough so that by glancing *up* she could tell that he'd begun to shave, something all three of her brothers aspired to, even James, who was seventeen. She found her tongue tangling a bit and didn't want to appear totally gauche. "Uh, where is your dog?"

"He's not mine. He's Old Vi's. Here, Tiger."

He turned back toward the kitchen door, and Rebel gaped at the animal that filled the opening.

"What is he?" she asked as Pookie forgot his dishes and began—perhaps unwisely—to bark. "Part horse?" Rebel guessed, only half kidding.

"Irish wolfhound. He's only a year old. Old Vi says he'll flesh out considerably this next year. My sister had a pony when she was little that was almost the same size. He's Tiger because of the brindle coat, sort of stripy. Trouble is, he has the disposition and the courage of a kitten, not a tiger."

Tiger regarded her and the yapping beagle at her feet with kind, compassionate dark eyes. Rebel realized she was melting; was it the dog or the boy?

She put out an explorative hand and held it quite still while the gigantic dog sniffed it, then licked at it.

He stood three feet tall at the shoulder and obviously weighed considerably over a hundred pounds. Again it was as if Moses replied to her unspoken question. "Irish wolfhounds are the biggest dogs in the world. He'll probably be one hundred and fifty pounds when he's full grown."

Pookie was still making small excited sounds, while the larger dog regarded him impassively. Rebel bent down to pick up Gram's dog and cautiously approached Tiger with him firmly in hand. "Pookie, meet Tiger. You're new housemates, looks like, so get acquainted."

The two dogs touched noses, and Pookie finally stopped barking. "Truce," Moses said. "I think you can set him down now. Tiger's not likely to be aggressive."

After waiting a few seconds to ensure the validity of this, Rebel brought up the other subject that had arisen over the past few minutes. "Why do you call your grandmother Old Vi?"

"Because she's Viola—Old Vi—and my mother's Young Vi—for Vivian. Less confusing, so I call her the same thing everybody else does." He hesitated, then said as if expecting condemnation, "She's kind of flaky, most of the rest of the family thinks."

"That's why she fits in with Gram. My family considers her a flake too."

"Buying this mausoleum," Moses said.

"Right. It might work, though. It's kind of a neat old

house, and it's not far from the university. They say there's a shortage of student housing. I hope it works so my dad won't have an excuse to say 'I told you so.'"

"My dad's big on 'I told you so' too. He's already telling me, and I haven't even done any of the things he's warning me about. I intend to, though, no matter what he says."

Intrigued, Rebel found a pan in a kitchen cupboard, compared it to the size of the Irish wolfhound, and searched out another larger one, handing it to Moses to fill with dog food. "Sounds like he has plans for you that you don't want to fall in with. Like my whole family is musical and I refused to learn piano. I knew, at three and again at six, that I had no musical talent whatever. So what does your family expect of *you?*"

"What would make him happiest would be to have 'Edgar Adams & Son, Attorneys at Law,' painted in gold on his office door." Moses made a snorting sound. "I can't imagine anything I'd rather do less than be a lawyer. Boring, boring, boring. He's not much interested in sports, but he'd even rather I played basketball than set my sights on writing, directing, and producing movies."

Rebel, who had some interest in writing stories herself, watched Tiger eat, holding the dish in place with one enormous paw. "What kind of things do you want to write?"

"Horror movies. Suspense. Trash, as my father would term it." Moses glanced around the old-fashioned kitchen where unopened gallon cans of paint on a counter suggested they would soon be painting the walls yellow. "I love trash, don't you? Spooky, scary books and movies. I like having the hair raised on the back of my neck and breaking out in goose pimples and getting a dry mouth and suspending my breathing because it's so *creepy*."

Rebel's tastes had always run more to romantic fantasy than to horror. However, Moses' enthusiasm—and the fact that she was rapidly evaluating him as *very attractive*, as well as taller than she was—was moderately contagious. "Ummm," she said, leaving him to interpret this however he liked.

"If he realizes that I'm not going to knuckle under to being a lawyer—which he will as soon as it's time for me to start college—he'll probably cut off all my funds. He says it's stupid to plan for something that doesn't guarantee me a living. I say it's stupid to plan for anything I don't enjoy doing, and that I can work at something else for a few years until I can earn a living making movies. He doesn't realize that the reason I agreed to come help Old Vi is that this place is a natural for a horror film. I don't have it written yet, but I'm working on it. You ever done any acting?"

Taken aback, Rebel said, "Not exactly. Just for myself; not on the stage or in a movie. I sort of like to act out my own stories when I'm alone."

"You make up stories too?" His smile widened. "You've got the right face for an actress. Good bone structure. Geez, Tiger, stop slopping everything all over the floor!" He made a dive for a roll of paper

WILLO DAVIS ROBERTS

towels standing on the counter beside the paint cans.

Stunned by the unexpected compliment, Rebel was reminded that she, too, had a puddle to clean up. "I think I'd better take Pookie out for a walk before he has another accident."

"Give me a chance to grab my video camera and I'll bring Tiger and drag him along," Moses suggested. "I don't pass up a chance to get any file footage that might be worked into a story."

Rebel hesitated for a moment, watching as Moses swiped more or less effectively at the mess Tiger had made.

She had decided, at about age ten, on what she hoped to find one day in a mate. Not that she was already looking, at her age, but Rebel always enjoyed thinking ahead. Then when something happened, you knew whether it was important to you or not.

As a girl, she knew she eventually wanted to marry and have a family. Ever since the days she'd started school, however, she'd been the tallest girl in her class. Even her teachers made that obvious in the way they were always having the kids line up according to height, and there was Rebel Keeling—who refused to answer to Amanda, and all through school each teacher who tried to call her that found him/herself ignored—at the head of the line. Looking down on all the lower heads. Hating the fact that even in kinder-garten she was aware that boys liked girls who were shorter than they were.

So by the time she was ten, she knew that she had

to stop growing (that hadn't happened until just recently, when it was already too late for normal height) or find an extraordinarily tall boy. That was only one of her requirements. The boy had to be smart, preferably as smart as or smarter than herself. He had to have a sense of humor. Her brother James had already convinced her that a male without humor was a pain in the butt. He had to have a sense of adventure and not ask stupid questions like, "Why on earth would you paint yourself *green?*" rather than helping her figure out how to get the paint off without taking her hide with it. And he had to be *interesting*. That meant liking to read and to learn new things, see new places, be brave enough to tackle things other people never thought of. That meant brightening when she made an outrageous suggestion instead of telling her flatly, "No way," for fear that trying something promising would lead to disaster. Sometimes it did, of course, but Rebel never planned to die of boredom. It was something she and Gram had in common.

And here before her, in his size sixteen Nikes that sort of got in his way as he tried to sop up the water around them, was a boy who had at least one of the attributes she'd always been watching for.

He was taller than she was.

Who knew how well he might qualify in the other specifications she'd settled on and been fine-tuning since she was ten?

Even Rebel couldn't have imagined how close he would come.

WILLO DAVIS ROBERTS

3

It was a beautiful, warm Seattle summer evening. Gram, who also enjoyed the high desert country of New Mexico, where she had lived for several years a long time ago, said one of the nicest features of Washington State was that having the Pacific Ocean surging onto its western coast and Puget Sound lapping along its inland waterways made the whole place air-conditioned.

Rebel had packed primarily to work at rather dirty jobs, but she was glad she'd come over to the new-old house in her best jeans and a pretty T-shirt that had colorful embroidery on it. She called out to Gram, who was doing something upstairs, to explain why they were leaving the house, and they started out.

After a momentary tangling of leashes—Pookie was excited at being taken for a walk, and Tiger was reluctant to go at all unless dragged—they headed for Forty-fifth, toward the university grounds. When Tiger suddenly decided to make a deposit on someone's manicured lawn, Moses whipped up the camera dangling from a strap against his chest and filmed the event.

Yechh, Rebel thought. *What kind of movie is he writing, anyway?*

"Can't think how this will be useful, but my intuition says don't waste anything," he remarked. "Trouble is, I forgot to bring my plastic bag. Maybe we'd better go where the property owners won't notice we're walking dogs."

"I have plastic gloves and bags, but I don't know how long they'll last with something that big," Rebel observed ruefully. "I'm prepared for Pookie-size stuff."

It wasn't her favorite job, but she was obviously stuck with it. Moses actually volunteered to scoop up after Tiger, but his hand was too big for the plastic gloves Rebel had stuffed in her pocket, and he was reluctant to do it without them.

"Okay, I'll be responsible this time. But this doesn't set a precedent for future walks," she was bold enough to say. She hoped there would be future walks. It was fun to walk along with a boy who was taller than she was.

It wasn't that she was embarrassed to be seen with a boy who was shorter. After all, this was the first taller one she'd ever encountered, and she enjoyed the company of boys. She had a couple of friends in school—the kids sometimes referred to them as the "Bobbsey Twins," who though not related were never seen

WILLO DAVIS ROBERTS

apart—who barely topped five feet five. While Rebel towered over them, she often sought them out because they were so funny. She had speculated that they liked being with *her* because the difference in heights was hilarious to everybody else, and the Bobbsey Twins had chosen as their purpose in life to keep everyone around them entertained.

Dad had taught her that a person's size shouldn't have anything to do with accepting him or her. "If you're lively, intelligent, and fun to be with, you'll have friends. And look at it the same way when you choose the kids you hang out with. If you rule out the ones who are too short or homely or awkward or shy, you'll miss some great people. In fact those are likely to be the most loyal best friends you'll ever have."

She enjoyed the Bobbsey Twins, even as she felt clumsy and awkward herself when they walked through the school hallways with her towering over them. Probably Tim and Phil, their real names, were embarrassed too, and wished they could make connections with some petite and pretty ladies who would make them seem tall by comparison. If so, they covered it well by cracking jokes, smiling at everybody (even the ones who made stupid remarks), and refusing to be drawn into confrontations with mouthy antagonists.

"They're only fourteen," Dad pointed out. "They've got lots of growing years ahead of them. Who knows. They may pass you up in a few years. Even if they don't, you'll all grow up and realize that height doesn't really matter to anyone who cares about you."

Rebel did realize that now, but it was still nice to walk with a tall guy.

Moses was taking pictures of everything as they went: a couple of little kids playing in a muddy spot they'd manufactured with a dribbling hose next to the sidewalk; an old woman working with her roses; an elderly couple rocking on their front porch as they watched the foot traffic and nodded, smiling, at the amateur photographer.

"File footage," Moses explained as he panned the neighborhood of enormous houses. "Evening is a good time. These places look shadowy enough to fit into a horror film. I don't know what I might need in the way of background stuff, but these houses are perfect. I'm going to get a lot on the house Old Vi invested in. Inside and out. How'd you like to pose for a few shots inside? Mysterious, seductive poses?"

Seductive? Me? Rebel wondered, awestruck.

"There's a building one street over," Moses was going on, oblivious to the fact that he'd touched a sleeping dragon inside her, previously only a harmless worm that liked to act out her own imaginings, "that belongs to my dad. He used to have his office there, in the old days, but my mom talked him into moving downtown when he could afford it. He didn't want to sell it, so it still belongs to him. It's rented out now, has a couple of apartments upstairs and on the bottom floor is a neighborhood grocery. It belongs to Mr. Dolzycki and it has a great deli. You want to check in and see what he's got leftover today that he might give us?"

"Sure," Rebel agreed as she stopped to disentangle the leashes again. The dogs kept crossing over each other, and it was impossible to stop them as long as she had to manage both of them. Moses needed both hands to operate his video camera.

They had turned the final corner and Moses indicated a storefront about a block ahead, focusing in on it. "I think I can work the deli into my story, and maybe Mr. Dolzycki, too. He's a colorful character. Has one of those big old-fashioned, handlebar mustaches, to make up for going bald on top. He's a good advertisement for his own food; he's short and round, and his wife is short and skinny. She makes up the deli stuff and he eats it."

"Isn't it getting kind of dark to keep taking pictures?" Rebel asked, giving a sharp jerk on Tiger's lead.

"No, they'll just look spookier. Good atmosphere. What's going on up there?"

In front of the store an old lady went sprawling, sending oranges and canned goods across the sidewalk. A middle-aged man in shorts and a golf shirt paused to help her up and rescue her groceries, while a younger individual in jeans and a T-shirt ran past them, directly into the focus of Moses' camera.

Moses never stopped filming, though he did demand, "What's going on?"

Just before the runner reached them, Pookie took objection to him and pulled sideways, dragging his own leash and the other dog with him, directly into the fellow's path.

The runner sprawled, swore, and scrambled to his feet.

Appalled, Rebel worked to get the dogs straightened out, trying to apologize. Moses, still filming, stepped on Pookie's foot, eliciting a pained yip. Tiger, his mass finally meeting its match in the runner, let out a few howls of his own.

Before she got everything straightened out—while Moses "helped" by filming the debacle—Rebel was on the ground herself, learning about Tiger's weight the hard way.

"For the love of Mike," she protested, "stop taking pictures and haul your dog off!"

Moses finally lowered video camera and let it hang from its strap. "Sorry. Come on, Tiger, sit! Not on *her*, idiot!"

Perhaps in protest at being so insulted, Tiger made a soft moaning sound.

"Tiger! Boy, did Old Vi miss the boat when she named you!" Moses was pulling on the leash, getting him well separated from the smaller dog and relieving the pressure on Rebel's foot. She sat for a moment, rubbing it. "She should have named you 'Fraidy Cat.' For your size, you're the biggest sissy I've ever seen."

"I guess it's not broken," Rebel decided, getting to her feet. "The real idiot was that guy who ran into us. How could he not have seen two people and two dogs right in front of him?"

"I think maybe he was looking back over his shoulder when he plowed into us." Moses lost interest in the inconsiderate runner. "Something's going on over at the store. Mr. Dolzycki's standing on the sidewalk, waving both arms. Better get him, too. Might be something useable."

Rebel accepted Tiger's leash again so that Moses freed both hands to work the camera. "Looks as if he's mad," she commented as they moved in the direction of the combined convenience store and deli.

The old lady who had been knocked down was sitting on the edge of the curb, nursing an injured elbow. Her rescuer, the younger man in shorts, had gathered her oranges and canned goods but looked apologetically at the store owner.

"Going to have to get another paper bag," he said. "This was torn all the way down."

Mr. Dolzycki was red faced and perspiring. "Young punk! 'This'd be a good place for a convenience store,' my wife said, 'and we'll put in a deli and cater to college students. They won't want to cook. They'll like my cooking,' she said. But do they want to pay for it? No, it's easier to steal what they want! Lately they been stealing me blind!"

Moses looked back the way they'd come. "Is that what happened? The guy who was running and knocked this lady down, he swiped something and ran away with it?"

"He broke my eggs," the lady sitting on the curb said, indicating the spreading yolks on the sidewalk. "When you yelled at him to stop, Mr. Dolzycki, he ran right over me and made me spill everything."

"I'll get you some more eggs. You want I should call a taxi to take you home, Mrs. Snelling?"

"No, no, I'll be all right in a minute. Who was he? Had you ever seen him before?"

Mr. Dolzycki scowled. "They all look alike. How can anybody tell? Stupid clothes, ridiculous haircuts, or *no* haircuts, ponytails on fellows who ought to be grown-up men, rings and studs in their ears or their noses or their belly buttons! Thanks for stopping to help, Mr. Henderson."

The Good Samaritan nodded. "No problem. You going to call the police?"

"What good would it do? I can't give a description of him. Could you, Mother?"

Mrs. Dolzycki, a mere wisp of a woman next to her husband, had come to the front door to look out at them. "I don't know. He looked a little bit familiar, but no, I don't think I'd ever seen him before. Most of our customers are nice young people, Papa. They don't steal; they're even polite. This one was just . . . strange. He actually bought a candy bar, then all of a sudden yelped and demanded his money back. I was just putting the money from Mrs. Snelling into the till and he grabbed it right out of my hand and took off with it. But he didn't give back the candy bar. Hello, Moses. Are you here to collect the rent? I mailed it, as usual, but I was a couple of days late."

The Dolzyckis went back inside, Moses following while Rebel stayed out front with the dogs. One brush of Tiger's tail could clear a lower shelf, so she didn't think he'd be appreciated in the building.

From her seat on the curb, Mrs. Snelling was saying, "I never got any look at him at all. He just plowed right into me, and down I went! Could you describe him, Mr. Henderson?"

"Uh—well. Not so very tall, not as tall as that young fellow." He directed a glance after Moses. "Just sort of medium in everything. I couldn't tell you the color of his eyes or hair. I was just so horrified that he'd knocked you down—"

From inside the store, wafting on assorted tantalizing odors, came Mrs. Dolzycki's voice. "He was a great tall thing—not as tall as Moses, but much taller than Papa. Dark, I think. Same thing they all wear these days: those blue jeans with holes in the knees and a T-shirt with something stupid written on it."

"It would help if you could remember what the something stupid was." Papa Dolzycki was scowling as he checked the eggs in a carton and prepared to take them out to his customer. "I didn't notice the holes in his knees. Or that he was particularly dark. Brown hair, I'd have said. Medium brown."

His wife regarded him soberly, her arms crossed over her chest. "So, do we call 911 or not? With at least three different descriptions, not much chance of catching up with him. What did he get away with? Only twenty dollars and a candy bar."

"Not worth the hassle of explaining it all to the police," Papa Dolzycki decided.

Moses was still filming, holding the video camera

to his eye. He paused over the deli counter. "What is that wonderful smell?" he asked, finally lowering the camera.

"We only got a few pastries left, and it's almost closing time. Why don't you and your friend"—here she glanced at Rebel—"take what's left in the case? We can't sell them tomorrow for fresh."

"If they taste as good as they smell, sure," Moses agreed. "Oh, this is Rebel. Her grandma's the one went in with Old Vi on buying the haunted house."

"First I've heard of it being haunted," Rebel observed. "It's not really, is it?"

"Sure looks like it could be," Moses said cheerfully. "I slept there last night, up on the top floor, and I heard things moving around. Breathing. Boards creaking. Stuff like that."

"The breathing was probably Tiger," Rebel suggested. "And all old houses creak."

Moses grinned. "You sleep in the attic tonight and see what you hear."

They accepted the bags of pastries—one of meat-filled pies, the other assorted sweet rolls—and left as the Dolzyckis were still exhorting Mrs. Snelling about taking a ride home rather than trying to walk.

"You're still pretty shaky," Mrs. Dolzycki told her, saying, "Good, good!" when the old lady gave in.

It had been long enough since she'd had supper that Rebel was ready to dive into the savory pies. The trouble was, trying to hold one to eat it while also juggling two dog leashes was virtually impossible.

WILLO DAVIS ROBERTS

"Look, you're going to have to stop making movies long enough for us to eat, so you can handle Tiger," she said, thrusting the leash at Moses. "What good are all these bits and pieces of ordinary things, anyway? What script are you following?"

"I'll be making it up, some of it as I go. Right now I'm just practicing, getting used to the camera, experimenting with lighting, et cetera. I'll get some ideas from the ordinary things, just in case nothing extraordinary happens except in my imagination. My dad always said I have too much imagination for my own good, though, so something will occur to me."

It was probably a good thing that Rebel didn't know just how much help Moses' imagination was going to get, nor that she'd be involved up to her neck.

4

Moses finally gave up on trying to film after it got totally dark except for street lamps. That way he could handle Tiger and leave Rebel with only Pookie and a pastry to manage.

The dogs smelled the food and had to be fed small bits from time to time, though Rebel was somewhat uneasy about this. "If I give him something that makes him sick, Gram will have a fit. Next time I'll remember to have a few doggy treats in my pocket. That is, if we're going to have a next time."

There. Might as well get it out in the open, so she wasn't left wondering.

"Good idea," Moses agreed, breaking off a bigger chunk of his pastry for the bigger dog, who swallowed it in one gulp. "Look at him! He couldn't even have tasted it before it went down! Yeah, I expect we've been nominated primary dog walkers in this ménage. You know what a ménage is?"

"A group living together in one household," Rebel said. "I don't get it. Both our grandmothers chose to have dogs, but at the first opportunity they push the responsibilities off onto someone else. Do you have a dog at home?"

"No." Moses licked his fingers, holding the paper bag upside down to demonstrate that it was now empty. Tiger sniffed at it and cried a little. "Yeah, buddy, I think so too. Good, but not enough of it. What's wrong with you now?"

For Tiger had stopped in his tracks—a considerable obstacle to further progress unless Moses threw some muscle into dragging him—and was now whining, looking off into a darkened yard filled with shrubbery.

As if to keep him company, Pookie began to bark.

"What's the matter? A squirrel still running around? Or a cat? More likely a cat. I can't let you chase it, boy, no matter what it is."

There were lights in the house, and the front door suddenly opened and an elderly man stuck his head out. "What's going on out there? What are you doing in my yard?" he demanded crossly.

"We're not in your yard, sir. We're out on the sidewalk," Moses told him. "We're just walking our dogs, and we haven't let them into your yard. See?" He pulled the flashlight out of his pocket and swung its arc over the dogs to demonstrate where they were. That didn't stop them whining and barking, though.

"I heard somebody in my yard. Right through those bushes. Made 'em brush against the window."

"Well, it wasn't us, mister. Something made the dogs bark, but we haven't been off the sidewalk,"

Rebel said. "Sorry if our dogs disturbed you. We think maybe they're barking at a cat."

"Bigger than a cat," the householder said sourly, not believing them. "A cat wouldn't have made the bushes move that high up. What's that thing around your neck, young man? What are you doing?"

"It's a video camera. Until it got too dark I was taking pictures. Nothing illegal. Sorry our dogs bothered you. We'll just take them on home," Moses promised.

That was easier said than done. The dogs didn't want to cooperate. It was possible to force Pookie to come along, though he continued to add his voice to the deeper one of Tiger's, who was definitely indicating that he wanted to go after something.

The walk seemed farther getting home than it had coming. In the areas between the corner streetlights, it was dark enough so Moses kept the flashlight on to keep from tripping over the elevated places in the sidewalks where trees had grown through.

Not until they'd turned onto their own street did the dogs finally quiet down. There were still sweet pastries in the second bag, and they showed renewed interest in that, but Moses decided they'd had enough. "We'll eat these when we get home and can shut you in the back room," he told Tiger, speaking to him as if the big dog could understand every word.

While they were gone, Viola had turned up. She had a newer car than Gram's, a rather classy-looking dark Buick sedan. They'd met before, but Viola reintroduced herself.

"Might've known you'd have found something to eat," she said, reaching for the paper bag. "Ah, been over to Dolzyckis', I see! Boy, you are never going to stop growing if you don't stop eating so much."

"I would surely like to stop," Moses admitted. "Growing, I mean." He helped himself to a frosted creation that oozed some kind of purple juice as the bag was passed around. "But there has to be a better way than starving in the meantime. Do you want him to have any of that, or do you want me to give him a biscuit? He's already had his share of the pastries."

Gram inspected the goodies and helped herself as well. She got a milk carton out of the refrigerator. "Glasses in that cupboard over there, Rebel. Guess you two hit it off all right. I thought you would."

She could have told me ahead of time that Moses was six and a half feet tall, Rebel thought, getting down the glasses before she made her own selection. "I've noticed there's no dishwasher in this kitchen, Gram. I hope I'm not expected to be the dishwasher as well as the dog walker."

"Don't look at me," Moses said. "I did a two-month stint at it last summer at a camp for crippled kids, and I promised myself that I'd never do it again. At least not for anybody who is able to stand on his or her own two feet."

"Got a dishwasher being installed next week," Gram said complacently. "In the meantime we'll use paper plates. Got a big stack of them right over there. You kids get to look over the whole house yet? Pick your rooms? Viola and I are temporarily in the back bedrooms down here on the lower floor. When we get everything decorated upstairs, we'll change, but for right now you can pick any room you like."

"I'm on the third floor. In the garret. A garret's an attic," Moses explained, making Rebel scowl faintly.

"I know what a garret is. Where a starving artist paints his pictures or the freezing, ragged writer types out with two fingers his priceless novel that's going to be a best-seller . . . or a movie."

"I'm a good fast keyboarder," Moses informed her, "not a hunt-and-peck typist. I brought my computer with me. You want a tour of the upper two floors, see which room you want?"

It seemed as good an idea as any. As they started toward the stairs, Gram called out, "We start painting here in the kitchen at eight o'clock in the morning, so if you want to eat, come down before that."

"She's not going to be a slave driver, is she?" Moses asked as they walked side by side up the wide stairway. "One reason I agreed to come and help was to get away from my father for a couple of weeks."

"She never has been before," Rebel responded. "Isn't there a light up here?"

"Yeah, but the switch is at the top of the stairs. Right over there. You have to take a few steps in half-light before you can reach it."

"Handy," Rebel grunted. "You already checked out all the rooms on this floor? Any reason you didn't pick one of them?"

"I like to play music late at night. I figured on the third floor maybe nobody would complain."

"What kind of music?" Rebel asked, suddenly suspicious. Had she avoided going to Salzburg only to buy into more of the same right here?

"Jazz is my favorite. I couldn't bring all my oldies, but I brought a few CDs and a radio. Am I going to get complaints if I listen to jazz at two A.M.?"

"Not from me," Rebel said, reassured. "Boy, even with the lights on, it's hardly daylight up here, is it?"

Moses squinted at the ceiling fixture. "I think that's about a twenty-five-watt bulb. I didn't think they still made them that small. I told Old Vi I'd put in some decent bulbs if they'd get some. There's only one bathroom on this floor—that door right there. So if you want to be close to that, pick a room on either side of it."

Rebel peeked into the bathroom, groping again for a light switch. "Wow! Straight out of the 1890s, wouldn't you say? A tub on feet. Is the water heater archaic too? Or can you actually have a hot bath?"

"Yeah, it's practically new. I think they're going to put a shower stall in that corner, but maybe not in time to do us any good. Check out that laundry chute. If we'd had one of those at our house when I was little, one of my brothers would have dropped me down it on my head and left my blood-spattered body at the foot for my mother to find. It's about thirty feet to the bottom, with a concrete floor."

"You've got brothers too? How many?"

"Two. Chet's twenty-two and Kevin is nineteen. They're both monsters. They agree with my dad that wanting to make movies for a living is a stupid aspiration. But they're smart enough so neither one of them wants to be his legal partner. And there won't be any more sons, so it's up to me. Except that I'm not going to be one either."

"What do they want to be?" Rebel asked, fascinated with this look into someone else's family background.

"Chet's a premed student at U-Dub. Kevin's got his eye on a psychiatric degree. You ever hear how many psychiatrists go into that because they need the therapy themselves? Kevin to a T."

"And you mentioned a little sister, too?"

"Sheila. She's eight. Sheila's okay. She plans to be a veterinarian and work with big animals and wild ones, like elephants and bears. She got to help sedate a grizzly once when it had to have a tooth pulled, and that decided her, right there. My folks think she'll outgrow it, and if she doesn't, they'll try to talk her out of it, but my money's on Sheila. They are even letting her keep a tarantula for a pet, thinking that will get her over her weird ideas, but it won't."

"A tarantula. I wouldn't mind having one for a pet. My folks say we're too busy to take responsibility for pets, and we take these fabulous vacations because Dad's an associate professor at the community college and has long summer vacations. We're not home enough to take care of dogs or cats. Do you have any pets?"

That was another requirement she ought to have added to her list for a potential husband. She knew her mother would be horrified that at fourteen she was thinking such thoughts, but after all, a girl had to start considering such matters eventually, didn't she? And Grandma Clara's opinion was that it was pointless to date any guy who didn't match up to your own standards, because the whole thing was aimed toward marriage and you didn't want to fall in love with someone who didn't meet them. Gram's theory was that it was a good idea to meet and become friends with a lot of people, and then choose the best from among them after you'd developed enough sense to do it. Rebel's own inclinations lay somewhere in between those two viewpoints.

"I had a golden retriever," Moses said, his voice going notably husky. "He was Kevin's, really, but after Kev left for college, I sort of inherited him, and he'd been my buddy before that. We had to put him to sleep about a month ago. He was pretty old, and he got so sick—" He cleared his throat. "So until I make up my mind what kind of dog I want, I don't have one."

"But your folks won't object if you get another one."

"No. They both like dogs. Mom thinks they're preferable to tarantulas, anyway. I don't know if she'd hold still for a twelve-foot long anaconda. Sheila has a friend who has one of those."

They had walked along the second-floor hallway,

peeking into various rooms. "They're all sort of furnished. More or less," Rebel observed. "Nothing fancy about any of them."

"They each have a bed, except for some of the ones up on the third floor. Some of them have a chair or a desk. Most of them have one of those things you use instead of a closet—a chifforobe? Chiffonier? All the closets were added long after the house was built. My dad came over and looked at the house before Old Vi signed the papers, and he thinks they're crazy to buy such an old place. But she says it's stood here for more than a hundred years, so why won't it stand another ten or two, until she's really ready to retire and be an old lady." He snorted. "Old Vi is *never* going to be a typical old lady, if you ask me."

"Gram, either. Or maybe they are typical of more people their age than our folks think. They're remembering their grandparents, who baked cookies and knitted through their old age. This one looks like it's been dusted, maybe. Guess I'll stay here," Rebel decided, choosing a room that overlooked the backyard.

Moses grinned a little slyly. "You sure you want to be the only one on the second floor? All by yourself?"

"Sure. Why not? I saw the curtains twitch when we were coming in, but that was you looking down on us, not a ghost."

He laughed. "Okay. Remember, both grandmas are practically deaf and they'll be a long way down, and not under this room, though. I mean, like if you scream or anything."

"I don't expect to scream," Rebel told him firmly. "I'll haul my suitcase up here."

"One thing I like," Moses approved, "is an independent female. Carries her own luggage, doesn't scream if something comes at her in the night."

As they made their way back downstairs, leaving lights on above them, Rebel asked frankly, "What other criteria do you have for females?" Maybe Moses, too, had his idealistic list for a potential mate.

"Somebody smart. My uncle, who's only an inch shorter than I am, says tall men are secure enough to marry women who are smarter than they are. He did. His wife's a physicist and speaks seven languages."

"Really? What does *he* do?"

"Anything he feels like at the moment. He trained as a lawyer, didn't care much for it, went into law enforcement. He's a beat cop and loves it but is debating whether he'd like to take the test for detective and see how he likes that."

"Interesting. Incidentally, is his wife tall, like he is?"

They reached the bottom of the stairs and headed for the kitchen, where there was still a light on and voices over Pookie's barking. Moses was grinning again.

"No. Actually, she's five feet five. But Uncle Glen has another saying. You know the old one about where does a bear sleep? And the answer is 'anywhere he wants to.'"

"I thought it was a gorilla. But in either case . . . what's it got to do with your uncle's wife?"

The grin broadened. "He says a smart man can pick any woman he wants, brainy or not, petite or not. I guess that's his philosophy about a lot of things. He can do whatever he chooses, as long as it's not illegal or immoral, whether he's a cop or not. What is the matter with that confounded dog?"

They emerged from the long hallway into the more brightly lit kitchen as Gram picked up her beagle and stroked his small head. "I don't know, he's been fussing ever since you brought him home. Sweetie, what is wrong with you? You can't need to go outside again now, after all that long walk."

Tiger, leaning against Viola's knee as she sat at the table with a glass of milk, whined sympathetically, deep in his throat.

"They're just getting used to a different house, different people," Viola guessed. "You find a room you like, Rebel?"

She shrugged. "They're all pretty much alike. I took the one at the back of the house, over the kitchen. I'm about ready to go up and go to bed." She frowned a bit at the dogs. "Do you think maybe we *should* take them out again, just for a minute? Is the backyard fenced so we can turn them loose out there?"

Even in Gram's arms, Pookie continued to emit small yipping sounds. "Maybe so. Just make sure the gate is secure before you let them loose," Gram decided. "It's on the north side of the yard."

It was a fairly sizeable space; Rebel could determine

that in the light that poured through the rear windows. And the fence was a solid wooden one, a good five feet tall. Rebel checked the latch on the gate before depositing the dog on the ground.

Pookie immediately took off into the dimness beyond the pale rectangles of light, sniffing and barking more freely.

"Nutty dog," Moses offered from the porch steps, which was as far as he'd ventured.

"Tiger's not much better. He's acting like there's something out here too."

"Yeah. I guess they always have to check out new territory. We don't have to stand around out here waiting for them to do their business, do we?"

"Don't see why," Rebel said, giving up on the erratic antics of the little dog and the much bigger one. "Gram can let them in when she's ready to go to bed."

She'd secretly hoped Moses would give in to chivalry and offer to carry up her luggage after all, but he didn't. He'd gone to work assembling the brushes, pans, and rollers for their job in the morning and spreading out newspapers all over the kitchen floor in lieu of tarps, though there were several of those to put over the counters and table and chairs later.

Rebel hauled her own baggage, leaving the light on in the second-floor hallway for Moses, who would be coming later. It wasn't until she'd had a bath in the big claw-footed tub, regretting the lack of a shower but grateful for hot water that spewed out of the ancient faucet, and retired to her new room that it struck her how accurate Moses' appraisal had been.

She didn't know if she'd ever slept alone on one floor of a house before. At home there had always been older brothers. Sometimes they'd been absolutely silen___ ___tened to t___ ___ticing them ___ ___versa-tions

T___ ___letely silen___ ___floor; Pook___ ___ge he was p___

It ___ slept in Gr___ ___dered if he'___ ___rters, then ___ ___gest. Pookie was, after all, Gram's companion, not hers.

She'd brought a few books to read before she went to sleep, but she didn't feel like reading tonight. She decided to turn out the light and just think over the evening, which had been different from the usual sit-and-watch-TV-or-read evenings at home.

The house was fascinating in its own way. Viola was a contrast to Gram, though they shared a lot of the same characteristics. They both met Moses' criterion of independent females. Neither of their families had felt that investing in a more-than-hundred-year-old house was a sensible thing to do, yet they'd relied on their own judgment.

Rebel, too, would trust her own judgment, no matter how old she got.

She heard Moses come up the stairs, and she thought about how it had felt to walk along the street with a boy who towered over her. The thin strip of subdued light under her door went out a few moments after she heard him continue on up the stairs, and then she detected the distant closing of a door.

Why did he need to close his door if he was all by himself up there? Who was going to surprise him?

What did she care? Rebel rolled over onto her side and let her memories play back, of walking the dogs with tangling leashes so Moses could operate his video camera. Of being knocked over when that idiot who stole a candy bar tripped over the dogs. Of meeting the Dolzyckis, sharing the pastries that would not be fresh enough to sell tomorrow, walking home to the big old-fashioned house where dozens and dozens of people must have lived before them.

What were their stories? Had any of them died in this house?

It was an unwelcome thought, but it stood to reason that *somebody* had died here in a hundred years.

Not in this bed. The bed wasn't that old. Well, of course that didn't mean anything. A person could have passed on any time up to the day Gram and Viola moved in.

She flopped over onto her other side. She was kind of sorry her family was leaving the day after next for Europe. She was eager to see how they would react to

Moses—and he, to them. How important was it that they liked one another?

Quite, maybe. They said when you married a person, you married a whole family of relatives.

Not that she was considering marrying Moses, of course. It was much too early for that. Still, it didn't hurt to stay on the alert and learn to evaluate the important things.

It wouldn't hurt to let her thoughts tickle away into what might be promising dreams.

WILLO DAVIS ROBERTS

5

Rebel lay for a moment, waiting for full conscious-
ness to come, for Gram to do something about
the dog.

Pookie yapped on.

Why had she ever thought she wanted a puppy?
Maybe her folks were right; they *were* a lot of trouble.

After a few minutes Rebel reluctantly swung her
legs out of bed and got up. She hadn't thought either
Gram or Viola was deaf enough to sleep through
the racket. She turned on a light, padded out into the
hall and found that switch so unhandily located, and
started down the stairs, turning on lights as she went.

It was raining. She could hear it slashing against the
windows and the wind rising in a way that made the
house creak around her. It had stood for a hundred years;
it wasn't likely to collapse now, she reminded herself.

She reached the ground floor and stood for an
uncertain moment in the lower hallway, trying to
remember which was her grandmother's bedroom and
which belonged to Viola.

That one, she thought, and cautiously turned the knob.

A gentle snore emanated from the darkened room. "Gram?" she said, and then realized the intermittent barking wasn't issuing from here. "He's in the kitchen," Rebel muttered, turning toward the sounds.

The kitchen door was closed, and Pookie was undoubtedly behind it. His little toenails scratched with some urgency, demanding to be freed.

"If you act like this every night I'm surprised she puts up with you," Rebel said crossly, easing open the door.

The little beagle was through the crack so fast it was only luck that enabled her to catch him. "No, no, now stop it," she said. Against her chest, the dog's heart was racing, pounding audibly. "What's wrong with you? Why are you making so much noise?"

"I shut him in the kitchen because he refused to stretch out and go to sleep," Gram said behind her, and Rebel swung around to face her. "He wanted to get into bed with me, and I wouldn't let him."

"Do you usually? Did you ever? I've heard that even once can be fatal. If you let them get away with it one time they figure from then on it's okay."

"Never. He has his own rug, beside my slippers. I even let him chew on them a little, training him to stay there."

Gram was wearing a T-shirt-type sleeping garment with the Twenty-third Psalm on it, somewhat faded from many washings. "I didn't think anybody'd be kept awake if I left him out here," she said. "I forgot you said you took the room directly overhead. I went right to sleep once I got him out of my room." She reached out to take the dog and cradled him, torn between compassion and annoyance. "You've always been such a good dog. Why are you behaving so badly now? We slept here last night, too, remember? And you slept just fine."

"What's going on?" Viola's sleepwear was a set of purple satin shorty pajamas. *They are cute*, Rebel thought, *but somewhat incongruous on a skinny old lady with knobby knees and varicose veins*. Viola emerged from her bedroom while fitting in her teeth. Gram, at least, still had her own and didn't have to take them out for the night.

"Oh, this fool dog wouldn't quiet down for the night and woke everybody up. What the heck is the front door doing standing open?"

Rebel, who'd had her back to it, spun around, startled, aware now of the cool damp wind blowing into the entryway. "I'd swear it was closed when I came down a minute ago," she muttered, wondering if she'd been awake or still half asleep when she reached the bottom of the staircase. "It must have blown open when the storm came up."

As if to verify this, another gust of wind swirled toward them, disturbing the stack of newspapers gathered for the next painting project and sending them scurrying to paste themselves against everybody's bare legs.

Suspicion suddenly made Rebel look up the stairs.

There was nothing visible, but she was remembering how Moses had grinned and made sly references to ghosts. Had he come down and opened the door? Playing tricks along the lines of a haunted house?

Before she could voice that thought, Moses himself appeared at the top of the stairs. He didn't have his glasses on, though they dangled from one hand. He was wearing only a pair of bright red gym shorts, which made Rebel conscious of her own worn pajamas, not covered by a robe. They were little-kid pj's, something Gram had picked up at a yard sale, and not what she'd have chosen to exhibit to an attractive guy.

For a boy who didn't have any athletic inclinations, he had nice muscles, she noted. She hadn't included impressive abs and thighs on her list of desirables in a mate, but at that moment it seemed worthwhile. There was something to be said for a man in healthy physical condition.

Her faded pajamas, too short at the ankles the way everything was always too short on her unless it had been ordered from a tall-size catalog, didn't reveal anything, but they didn't enhance her appearance, either. Rebel tried not to cringe visibly.

"I was sure I locked that door," Viola said, frowning as she closed it now, pushing against the force of the wind.

"I locked it too," Gram offered. "Hmm. Maybe one of us locked it and the other one *unlocked* it."

Moses came the rest of the way down the stairs. "Did either one of you slide the bolt?"

Nobody had, or at least they didn't remember it. They weren't used to needing to use bolts in addition to the regular twist locks, and nobody could remember whether it meant a door was locked or unlocked when you turned the button flat across or straight up and down.

Gram finally put Pookie down, and he immediately raced to the now definitely locked door and smelled all along its base, beginning to bark again.

"Oh, for goodness sake! Nobody'll ever get any rest tonight," Gram said exasperated. "What do I have to do, rock him to sleep?"

Moses glanced into the surrounding shadows where the overhead light scarcely penetrated. "Speaking of sleeping, where's our oversize watch dog? Don't tell me Tiger slept through all this. I heard you all the way up in the attic."

"He was on the rug beside my bed," Viola said, turning toward her room. "Here, Tiger! Are you here?" They scattered to search for him.

A few moments later they were all once more assembled in the front hall, staring at one another. Tiger was nowhere to be found.

Viola, alarmed, insisted on getting dressed and going to look for him.

Moses, unwilling to let her go out in the storm alone in the middle of the night, got dressed and improvised some foul-weather gear from plastic garbage bags. "Wait a minute. I'm going with you," he insisted.

With Pookie back in Gram's arms, Rebel held the

front door open and yelled into the night. "Tiger! Here, Tiger! Come!"

She hadn't brought a coat of any kind from home, and the driving rain, though not especially cold, wasn't inviting. Gram didn't have a coat either, certainly not anything waterproof. It hardly ever rained hard enough in the summer in Seattle to make anyone prepare for such a thing.

Half an hour later both Viola and Moses were back, drenched in spite of their makeshift slickers. "Tiger's never been allowed to run loose in the city," Viola said, shivering as she peeled off the wet plastic and dropped it in a heap on some of the newspapers. "He's never run away before, either, and I don't know if he can deal with city traffic."

"There isn't much this time of night. He might get lost, though." Moses gave Rebel a significant look. He didn't think too much of Tiger's intelligence, for all that he was a splendidly handsome animal.

Viola was near tears. "I can't bear to just go to bed and leave him out there without knowing what's happening to him. Is that why Pookie was making such a fuss? Because Tiger got loose, and *he* didn't?"

"But the door wasn't open when I came downstairs. I couldn't have walked past it with the wind and the rain blowing in and not noticed it. And Pookie was still locked in the kitchen then," Rebel remembered.

"Maybe Tiger got loose in the backyard, not out the front way." As soon as she thought of that possibility, Viola went to yell out into the fenced backyard, but there was no sign of the big brindle-striped Irish wolfhound. Directly across from her the deserted dining room was a black hollow, with no dog in it.

None of it made any sense. But neither did standing around waiting for morning. They might as well try to get some sleep.

"I wonder if I shouldn't call the police," Viola said, blowing her nose.

"You can contact the animal-control people in the morning. He has a collar, and ID on it, so if anybody finds him, they can track you down at your vet's. Come on, let's go back to bed, and we'll look for him when it gets daylight," Moses urged.

Without discussing it, the mutual decision was made. They wouldn't start painting until they'd made an all-out effort to locate the missing Tiger.

The storm had blown itself out by morning, and the outside world, while glistening with moisture, had a welcome freshness about it under clear blue skies, heavy with the scent of blooming roses. "Shall we stick together or split up and cover more territory faster?" Rebel asked as she and Moses left the house.

"Well, Old Vi and your grandma have agreed to go together, for moral support, I guess, and they'll walk Pookie at the same time. Tiger's been gone for hours and apparently didn't have sense enough to find his way back here, so he probably won't. Maybe we'd better split up. I'll go east if you want to go west."

Rebel prayed they'd return home to find that the

animal-control people had found Tiger. He was, after all, a rather large animal not to be noticed. Surely someone would report him or see the number on his collar and call the vet's office.

Quite a few people were working outside in their yards, cleaning small branches and leaves blown down on their lawns. All of them were willing to pause and answer Rebel's questions, but nobody had seen a pony-size dog with a red collar.

She was debating how much farther to go when she recognized Mr. Dolzycki's deli and decided to go in and talk to them before she turned around.

The Dolzyckis remembered her and greeted her with wide smiles, though it seemed to Rebel that Mrs. Dolzycki's seemed a bit forced.

"Where is your friend today? That Moses, he is a nice boy. Can never fill him up. My boys, they're not so big, but they were just like that. Always eating! I miss feeding them, but Louie lives in Florida now, has his own air-conditioning business. And Tony moved away to southern California, for the climate! What's the matter with this climate, I'd like to know?"

"Nothing, usually, but that storm last night might have run off a few people. It *did* run off Moses' grandmother's dog, the big one we had when we came before. I don't suppose you've seen him this morning? Tiger?"

"No, no! He's lost, is he? Sorry to hear it. You've walked all that way again so soon. Why don't you sit down and try one of my strudels, and I have a few tidbits you can take for the dog. If he smells it, he'll come running."

Rebel perched on one of the stools at the deli counter to feast on the strudel, wondering if she should go back the way she'd come or try another route. Who knew where a lost and scared dog might go?

Mrs. Dolzycki turned to Rebel, bringing her a can of soda to go with her food. It was a wonder they made a living here, the way they gave away the merchandise. "When your grandmas are ready to rent the rooms, make a note and put it up on our bulletin board. The students advertise everything that way— bikes and cars for sale, looking for rooms or roommates. I'm glad I'm not having to do that. I picked my roommate fifty-two years ago." She glanced over at her husband, who was building a display of olive cans, and laughed. "I didn't do a bad job of it, either."

This was interesting. Rebel liked knowing how couples had met, so she could better imagine what her own experience might be. She knew her parents had both been college students when they met, and that they'd dated for over a year before Dad had proposed, though they'd known before that that they'd marry. Rebel had been only nine when she'd asked, "Was it love at first sight, Mom?"

"Heavens, no. But we liked each other's looks, and we worked up from there. Became friends and study partners, and finally knew we wanted to be partners for life."

Dad, grinning, had added to that, "And I got a job

that enabled me to buy a car. She sure liked that car. I think she fell in love with *it* at first sight."

When she'd asked Grandma Clara about her romantic life, her grandparent was happy to oblige with her own story. "We met in church. We sang in the choir together. We dated for two years, and then he proposed at a church picnic. We were married eight months later. It was lovely."

Rebel screwed up her face. "But if you were in love, why did you wait so long to get married? Didn't you want to get married right away?"

"Oh, my no. It was such fun to be engaged. It was a delightful eight months before we took on the responsibilities of marriage. We had a chance to save enough money for a down payment on a house, too. Houses didn't cost nearly as much in those days."

Disbelieving, Rebel had demanded of Gram the next time she saw her, "I thought meeting and getting married was supposed to be *romantic*. Doesn't anybody really fall in love at first sight?"

"Sure," Gram said at once. "Jerry and I did. You think your daddy's good looking, you ought to have seen his father." She smacked her lips, kissing her fingertips. "It was at the county fair, and I was nineteen years old and thinking I'd be an old maid forever. I'd had two proposals already, mind, but neither of them was anybody I'd have considered spending the rest of my life with, you understand. I was with my best friend, Lizzie Savekka. Neither of us had a boyfriend, though Lizzie'd been making eyes at Al Trentham. Anyway, we decided to take one more ride on the Ferris wheel before the evening ended, and who was operating it but Jerry Keeling. He was traveling with the carnival that came to the fair every year, and I thought he was the best-looking thing I ever saw on two feet." Gram smiled, savoring the memory.

This was more like it. Rebel smiled too. "And you fell in love with him right that minute? On the spot, the first time you saw him?"

"Well, I sure fell in *like*," Gram confirmed. "He grinned at us and teased us when we got on, and I kept watching him down below all the time we were on the ride. And when we got off, he took hold of my hand to help me, and oh, he was a smooth talker! Offered to buy me an ice cream if I'd stick around until closing time, which was only another twenty minutes. We had the ice cream, and talked for an hour, and I went home and told my folks I'd met the man I was going to marry."

"Did he propose that quick, then?" Rebel demanded.

"No, no, but I knew he was going to. My daddy wasn't exactly pleased that I was taking up with a carnival worker, and as handsome and sweet talking as Jerry was, even Mama thought I'd ought to take my time, think about it some. The carnival was in town a week, and I saw Jerry every day of it, and before it left town, he'd quit being a carney and found himself a job at the feed store. Two weeks later old Mr. Malvern had a stroke, and they made Jerry store manager because he knew more than anybody they'd have hired off the street, and the salary was enough to get married on. So we did." Gram's voice was rich with satisfaction.

"And you lived happily ever after," Rebel sighed, before she remembered. "Until he died."

"Well, I was devastated when he died, but it was a good, sound marriage—based on love and respect and fun. Don't ever even consider marrying anybody unless they're *fun*." She sobered. "I wasn't sure about Wes and your mom. They were sort of stuffy, you know. Didn't relax enough, didn't laugh enough. I guess Wes had too much responsibility too young, after his daddy passed on. He's loosened up considerably since you kids all came along."

"And you both knew it, right away, when you met. That the other person was special."

"Oh yes. No question about that. Knew it the minute I laid eyes on him. The only reason to marry any man, Rebel, is that you can't stand *not* to marry him and spend the rest of your lives together. I never wanted anyone else, after Jerry. Never met anyone who touched off such a spark. No, it was more like a conflagration."

This was a more satisfactory recital of facts. It gave Rebel hope that eventually she, too, would suddenly encounter a person who would turn her world around and become part of it forever.

And now Mrs. Dolzycki had said she'd been married for fifty-two years, announced with the coyness of a young woman. Her story, too, might be memorable.

Rebel sipped from the can, then chewed around another mouthful of the flaky pastry. "Did you and Mr. Dolzycki fall in love at first sight?" she asked.

"Oh, did we ever! One look, across a dance floor, and our eyes met, and we melted. Turned to soft butter inside." The odd little smile that hovered around the old lady's lips gave Rebel a twinge of envy, shaded by respect and admiration. "A waltz or a polka can still get my pulse to fluttering. You want another one of those, young lady?"

Rebel licked her fingers. "No, thanks, though it was wonderful. I'll tell Gram about putting up a sign on your bulletin board when the house is ready to rent out rooms. Now I have to go on hunting for Viola's dog. He's not used to running loose in the city and may not know how to dodge cars. Is it all right if I take the rest of the pop with me?"

Mrs. Dolzycki waved a hand. "Oh, of course! I know what it is to lose a beloved pet. We used to have a dog, but when he died—he was fourteen years old, very old for a dog!—we didn't have the heart to replace him. Now we don't have a watchdog anymore. You go find your Tiger."

Rebel thanked her for the tasty warm pastry and set out, trying not to be as dispirited as the others had been when she'd left them. Maybe one of them had found Tiger by this time. He might be rather timid, compared to Pookie, but she couldn't believe he wasn't smart enough to keep from being hit by a car in a residential area even if he was lost. If he hadn't wandered out onto one of the main arterials, where the traffic was really heavy, he'd have a good chance of surviving until somebody found him.

She decided to walk back by a different route, in case the dog had been frightened by the storm and run blindly into strange territory. The damage was the same here, several blocks over, with scattered branches, torn up flower beds, rose petals torn loose and scattered over everything.

Wherever she encountered anyone cleaning up the mess, Rebel paused to ask if they'd seen a huge brindle-striped dog.

"Didn't come out in the weather last night," one old man told her woefully, surveying what was left of his landscaping. "Wouldn't have seen him then. I heard a lot of banging going on when the wind was at its worst, just before midnight. I figured my metal garbage cans blew off the porch. They were empty, and sure enough, I can see one of them against my back fence. I haven't even gone out there to inspect the worst of it yet." His scowl deepened as he studied a muddy rut cut deeply into the wet earth of his lawn. "What do you suppose made that?"

In the ensuing silence, as they both tried to figure it out, Rebel heard a sound. A *familiar* sound.

She lifted her head, listening intently. "Tiger?" she called out, unsure where it was coming from. "Tiger, is that you?"

The whine was unmistakable. She didn't know how even a one-hundred-pound dog could have made the

WILLO DAVIS ROBERTS

tracks across the lawn, but instinct drew her to follow that trail.

The gate separating the frontyard and backyard had either blown open or never been closed in the first place. A large branch, big enough to have knocked down a grown man if it had fallen on him, had been dragged over the soft ground, gouging the tracks where two sharp broken lesser limbs had served as a two-pronged plow.

The main limb, too long to pass through the gate, had wedged in front of it. And on the other side of the fence, collar hopelessly snarled in the fallen branches, stood the most woebegone Irish wolfhound Rebel had ever seen.

When he saw her, he threw back his massive head and howled in a way that would have raised the hair on Rebel's head if she hadn't been so glad to see him alive.

6

"Well, I never saw a bigger dog than that!" the old man said, peering over Rebel's shoulder. "Boy, he's got himself in a mess, don't he? He couldn't get through the opening dragging all that stuff, and it plugged the hole so he couldn't get out again, either." He leaned forward to better evaluate the situation. "Might have to cut him loose from there. Easier than trying to disentangle him from here where we can't hardly even reach him. Maybe we better go through the house, come at him from the other side. Get something to cut that leash if we have to. I'm Ezra Merkin, by the way."

The minute they backed away from the open gateway, Tiger began to howl in earnest. He'd probably been trapped here for hours, ever since he got loose and lost, and he objected to Rebel leaving him.

She followed the homeowner up the front steps and into his house, which was almost as old as Gram and Viola's. It even had the same general floor plan, on a slightly smaller scale. A dim hallway led back to the kitchen, where they could hear Tiger's frantic efforts to escape from his prison of tree branches.

Rebel spotted a telephone on a counter. "Would you mind if I called home and told them I've found him?" she asked.

"Help yourself," the old man said, getting a large pair of scissors out of a drawer and heading for the back door.

Moses answered on the second ring.

"I found him. He's okay but caught in some debris that blew down. Two blocks north of the street where we walked over to the deli, in a pale pink house with white trim. Come help me get him home, and bring a rope or another leash if you can; we may have to cut this one to get him loose."

"Be right there," Moses said, and hung up, not wasting time. That might be a valuable trait in a husband, she thought in satisfaction. When she got ready to make such a decision, which would be years and years in the future, if her mother had anything to say about it.

Rebel followed the old man onto the porch and heard him muttering over the racket Tiger was making. "Well, would you look at that! Looks like somebody came through here and jumped up on the railing, left muddy tracks all over the place!"

Sure enough, both the rail and the porch deck had smudged foot marks in a distinctive pattern of loops and whirls. Man-size feet, Rebel decided, but not nearly a size sixteen.

Tiger, hysterical with hope at the sight of her again, was throwing his weight against his tangled leash, nearly strangling himself.

"No wonder I thought I heard things moving around out here. Will he bite if I try to get close to him?"

"I'm pretty sure not. But maybe it would work best if I got hold of him and you cut the leash where it's caught. That'll still give me something to hold on to," Rebel suggested. "It almost looks as if he was chasing somebody, doesn't it? And the guy cut through your yard and leaped up onto your porch to get away from Tiger."

"Could be. Let's see how we're going to do this now."

"Sit, Tiger. Sit and be still. You're just going to make it harder."

But Tiger was now wagging his tail in rhythm with the rise and fall of his moaning. It was not until Rebel dropped to one knee in the wet grass and wrapped both arms around the big dog that he finally subsided and licked at her face in gratitude.

She could tell he was trying to obey her command to sit and be quiet, but it was difficult for him. *Poor Tiger,* she thought. *Maybe he'd given up hope of ever being rescued.* She continued to try to calm the dog while her mind wrestled with the evidence.

They were still in the backyard, and the old man was hacking away the large portion of the tree that blocked the gateway, when Moses arrived. He had

Pookie's leash, tiny by comparison to the wolfhound's own, but decided that since they'd severed Tiger's lead close to the end, he could manage with that.

"Look at the footprints on the porch before we leave," Rebel urged.

"Some fellow with pretty big feet," the old man said, then glanced down at Moses' athletic shoes. "Well, way bigger than mine, anyway."

"About a twelve," Moses decreed with the certainty of one who'd worked his way well beyond that size. "Look at the side of the porch, where Tiger could reach it."

Rebel leaned over to look at it, fending off the dog's enthusiastic approval by licking at any part of her he could reach. That only ruled out her forehead when he stood on his hind legs and she lifted her chin as high as possible. "He clawed like crazy. Old Tiger was trying to get this guy, Moses. Nothing timid about him at all."

"Who was he?" the old man asked curiously, glancing from one young face to the other as they towered over him.

"We don't know, but we think maybe he was attempting to burglarize our house," Moses informed him. "The front door was accidentally left unlocked when we all went to bed, and when the guy opened it, Tiger scared him off and chased after him."

Mr. Merkin clearly found this quite diverting, waving them off when they thanked him profusely for his help.

"Haven't had so much excitement since my corn popper caught fire," he told them.

"You know," Rebel observed when they finally started for home, "that still doesn't quite explain everything. If Viola locked it and Gram unlocked it, the door still wasn't standing open when I came downstairs. So who shut it after the burglar left, or was he still lurking around and I went past him to let Pookie out of the kitchen? He was still having a fit when I went downstairs, trying to be a watchdog. And where was Tiger all this time? When did he chase our intruder outside? Why didn't he bark?"

"He never barks," Moses stated. "He whines. Whimpers. Moans. Never barks."

"Well, he must have tried to do his best this time. And for once you're not having to drag him into cooperating during a walk. I think he knows we're taking him home." She shivered just a little. "Do you think the guy might have been hiding in the dark dining room when I went past that door toward the kitchen? And gone out the front door and left it open behind him while I had my back turned? Only where was Tiger while that was going on?"

"Maybe the guy got in and Tiger moved on him, and he managed to open the front door and somehow get the dog out and then had to get out past him to escape and Tiger took out after him. If we ever catch this creep we'll have to ask him."

They were met by an ecstatic Viola, and Gram was much relieved, too. Tiger was quite willing to accept dog biscuits, water—though he'd been out in a pouring rain all night, there hadn't been any available to drink—and plenty of affection. Now the deep-in-throat moans he produced were clearly expressing pleasure.

"We fixed the lock on the front door so we won't make that stupid mistake again," Viola announced, finally rearing back so that her pet couldn't continue to wash her face with his large tongue. "We used nail polish to show that it's locked when the ridge on the button is up and down. So it won't matter who locks it—the other person won't unlock it without meaning to."

"Good thinking," Moses said, a classic understatement. "Did you figure out if the guy stole anything?"

"There wasn't much of anything to steal," Gram said. "We only moved in enough stuff to subsist on while we're getting the decorating done. We didn't bring much in the way of personal valuables. I'm ashamed now of the way I scolded Pookie and locked him in the kitchen. He was only trying to warn me, bless his little heart."

Pookie, who had also benefited from the dog treats being handed out to the larger dog, wagged his tail and accepted some petting as his due, a fellow hero.

"Well, they're not going to be able to explain everything that happened," Rebel said. "I'm almost hungry enough, after tramping for miles all over the U District, to eat one of those imitation hot dogs Pookie and Tiger are chomping. I don't suppose anybody thought of anything to have for lunch?"

"You'd suppose wrong," Gram said, grinning. "I put on a pot of chili, and there are fresh crackers and fruit." She cast a sly glance at Rebel. "Your mother called this morning to check on you, and I didn't want her to think I was just feeding you junk food."

"Why did she need to check on me?" Rebel asked, frowning. "I've only been gone from home for one night!"

"And once she leaves the United States she won't be able to call you as easily." Gram led the way toward the back of the house. "I didn't tell her you were searching for a lost dog. That would have entailed more explanations than I thought it wise to get into. I didn't want your folks to decide at the last minute that it was dangerous to leave you here. So I just told her you were walking the dog and let it go at that."

"You have a devious mind," Rebel told her grandmother admiringly as she got out the bowls for the chili.

It never occurred to Rebel that it might actually *be* dangerous to stay here in this old house. Only that it was going to be a lot of work, and they might as well get to it. Right after they'd polished off two bowls of steaming chili and a juicy nectarine apiece, they started on the painting.

It wasn't until long after they'd cleaned up for the day, admiring their newly pale yellow kitchen, that Moses made his alarming discovery.

"Hey, you want to look at the pictures I got last night?" he asked Rebel. "I must have that roll of film pretty well used up. Before you got here, I wandered all over the house taking spooky shots. Easy, with the crummy lighting in this place. Even when they're on, they leave a lot of shadows and dark corners."

"Sure," Rebel agreed.

A few minutes later, Moses was scowling. "I can't find my video camera. Didn't I set it down on that little table here in the front hall?"

"I didn't pay any attention." Rebel's eyes narrowed. "Say! If it was there, that would have been in easy reach for that burglar! Do you think we ought to call the police? Or at least tell your uncle who's on the Seattle police department?"

Moses made a sound that was remarkably like Tiger's moan. "It's not a new camera; it's one my Uncle Rog gave me when he got a newer one, but I can't afford to replace it. And my dad sure won't. He thinks all my moviemaking aspirations are stupid. I don't think it's even covered by our insurance, because Dad has a big long list of electronic stuff on the home-owners' policy, but not that. I had some good shots. Why would a stranger take that? It wasn't worth that much anymore. He probably could only sell it for a few hundred dollars."

Rebel had never seen anybody actually gnash his teeth before. It was rather interesting.

"Maybe he dropped it when he was trying to get away from Tiger. It might be worthwhile to go look for it."

"If anybody found it," Moses speculated, "they'd

pick it up and keep it. It's worth *something*. There's not much chance it would still be where he dropped it."

"Well, he went through some backyards, rough terrain for in the city. What if he dropped it when he ran through that clump of a tree that Tiger got stuck in? It could easily have been be lost. It's still daylight; why don't we have a look around?"

So they did. And the first thing they discovered, on their own back porch the same as it had been on Ezra Merkin's house where Rebel had found Tiger, was a set of muddy footprints.

Moses said a word that was very close to profanity, dropping to his knees beside the images that had now dried on the covered pale gray painted surface. "Recognize the pattern? I don't even need to look at the drawing I made of it. It's the same guy, Rebel. He was on the back porch here, too. Looks like he was trying to get in the rear of the house, and then he must have gone around to the front and found it was open."

"Or easy to open," Rebel countered. "I never picked a lock, but that one that's on the front door now looks to me like one of those you can open with a credit card, like they do in the movies. If you knew how."

Moses stood up, once more towering over her. "It's not hard. I saw my uncle do it when he got locked out of his house. It seems this guy really did want to get into our house, and Tiger really did chase him quite a ways. You'd think five or six blocks—isn't that how far away it is?—was far enough so ol' Tiger would have caught him."

"Maybe not, if he was already tangled up in that big branch and was dragging it with him. Maybe we ought to try to find where it came from."

There was a certain amount of satisfaction in putting their heads together, trying to make sense of it. And of course Moses had the added incentive of wanting to recover his camera, in addition to solving a puzzle.

They retraced what they thought might have been the route an intruder could have taken to have wound up where they'd discovered Tiger, asking questions door-to-door about the missing camera. Nobody admitted to having found one, but they did find the tree with the missing branches, only half a block from where it had stuck when the dog tried to go through a gateway.

The homeowner was grimly working with a chain saw on what remained of the tree. When they paused beside him, he was willing to rest for a moment to speak to them. "Wind brought down so much of it I might as well trim down the rest of it and start over," he said, wiping his forehead.

"We think our dog got caught in part of it and dragged it," Moses said, indicating the drag trail on the man's lawn. "There are more marks like this where he went into someone else's yard and tried to follow a thief through a gate, where he got hung up because of the branches he was caught in."

"A thief? He get something important?"

"My video camera. We're hoping that maybe the guy dropped it somewhere when the dog got close to him, and it was probably about the time Tiger was catching up with him. Would you mind if we looked around here, just in case?"

"Help yourself. Lot of stuff came down off the tree besides a big chunk that's missing. You might look through that pile," the man suggested. He stood still for a minute, watching them throwing broken branches aside, searching.

It was Rebel who spotted it, reaching down through rough, wet foliage that scratched her arm and her cheek to emerge triumphant. "It's here! He dropped it, maybe just before Tiger got tangled up and couldn't catch him!"

Anxiety showed on Moses' face. "I don't know what being out in the rain would do to it. Or if the film is still in it. Let's take it home and find out." He turned to the interested householder with his chain saw. "Thanks, mister."

"It's time we turned detective," Rebel suggested as they moved toward home. "Why did somebody break in and only steal a video camera?"

"The front door was accidentally unlocked and the camera was sitting just inside the hallway?" Moses speculated.

"There wasn't much else to steal," Rebel pointed out. "It's an almost empty, being-renovated house. And at some point Tiger caught on that there was an intruder in the place and took out after him. I haven't figured out when that was, though, because I know that front door was locked when I came downstairs."

"Closed," Moses corrected thoughtfully. "What if the guy tried to close it behind him, with Tiger at his heels, and it didn't latch? The next gust of wind blew it open again."

"If Tiger was after him, would he bother to try to close the door, though? Wouldn't he just take off running instead of worrying about shutting the door as he left?"

"Only if it was to put the door between him and Tiger. And we know Tiger got out, too. What if Tiger was already outside, and the thief was still inside the house when you came down, and he knew he had to get out in a hurry. He may have come in, grabbed the camera, and been surprised when Tiger came out of Old Vi's bedroom to investigate. You know Tiger—he doesn't bark at anything, just whines. He's big enough to be intimidating, but he's never made a move to bite anyone, so maybe the guy just tried to get out alone and Tiger outmaneuvered him. I'll have to think about how he'd have expected to manage that. What the thief thought, I mean, not what Tiger thought. I'm not sure he thinks," Moses concluded glumly.

He'd been inspecting the camera. "The film's still inside. Let's take a look. Yeah, if nothing's damaged by the rain it's all here. It looks like it could be pretty waterproof if it wasn't actually submerged. It landed off the ground in those branches where the water ran off."

"It makes you wonder if he broke in just specifically for the camera or expected to find something else valuable. How would anybody know there was a video camera to steal?"

"Well, I've been walking around the neighborhood for a couple of days, taking pictures of everything, so somebody could have noticed. And there was that guy who swiped the candy bar at the Dolzyckis'. He must have noticed I was filming him when he ran into us. If he stole candy, he might steal something else, too."

They approached the house side by side, and they had almost reached the front steps when Rebel paused, eyes narrowing. "What the heck is that?"

Crumpled against the side of the steep stairs that led to the small porch was a wad of dark blue material, which proved, when she reached for it, to be a sopping windbreaker. Moses put out a hand and lifted a section of it out to the side, displaying its pitiable condition.

"Got a sleeve almost torn off. Probably blew here during the storm. Maybe somebody threw it away in one of those garbage cans that were rolling around and had their lids knocked off."

Rebel peered at the cast-off garment more closely. "Moses, look at those holes. They could be teeth marks. See where they punctured the sleeve and then ripped some more? Big dog teeth, maybe?"

"Tiger?" Moses was incredulous. "Not likely. He's too timid to tackle a cricket."

"Maybe not. Remember those tracks on old Mr. Merkin's porch, and it was obvious Tiger was chasing him. Maybe our burglar was wearing this jacket, and

Tiger got hold of it and ripped it and the guy shrugged free of it and got away."

Still dubious, though maybe less so, Moses took the dripping windbreaker and held it up, spread out so that they could examine it better. "Man's. A lot smaller than I am," Moses pronounced. "It's kind of heavy. Check the pockets, see if there's anything in them."

The left pocket revealed a crumpled Mars bar wrapper.

The right one held something more substantial, and as Rebel drew it out, she gave an exclamation of expectation.

"Hey! We're in luck! The guy lost his wallet!"

7

Water oozed from the limp cheap leather wallet as Rebel opened it, anticipating a driver's license with a picture, a name, and an address.

To her vast disappointment, it contained nothing of the sort. Only in the inner fold did she find the money: four twenty-dollar bills. The top bill had a smear of red ink on it. Otherwise there was nothing special about it.

Moses scowled at them and the now offensive excuse for a wallet. "Maybe he's smart enough not to carry any ID when he pulls off a robbery."

"Not smart enough to keep from losing his jacket and this money. Your uncle's a police officer, Moses. But you don't have to be a cop to investigate the obvious."

"Okay, so what's the obvious?" he wanted to know.

"Well, we don't have our thief's picture, but we know his shoe size is about a twelve, and from this jacket"—Rebel twisted her mouth in thought—"I'd say he's about the same size as my brother Conrad. Say, 5 feet 9, 145 pounds. What do you think?"

Moses was nodding. "So far, so good. But how do we detect beyond that?"

"Tiger knows him." Rebel allowed herself a grin. "We could walk around and see if Tiger gives any sign of recognizing anybody. My bet is he's a college kid— or maybe a high school one—and we might find him at one of the local hangouts. Coffee shops, pool halls, places like that. Bars."

"They won't let us into the bars."

"We could stand outside and see who comes and goes."

"Late at night? That's when people are coming and going."

"Who would know? Gram and Old Vi go to bed early enough so there'd be a lot of time afterward. Who knows? We're tall enough to look older than we are. They might even let us inside some of those places, as long as we didn't try to buy anything to drink."

"Yeah. And we'd be really inconspicuous. We both tower over everybody else. Besides, which watering hole would we choose to stake out? There are dozens of them within walking distance of the U."

"I'll bet Tiger has a good nose. He might pick up the scent on the sidewalk outside if we made the rounds."

Moses draped the jacket over the porch railing to drip dry, retaining the wallet with the twenty-dollar bills in it. "It would take a pretty good nose. I wonder if there's any chance he'll try to come back and recover this stuff."

"Not likely in daylight, though we can keep an eye on it, just in case. Dogs do have good noses, a lot better than ours. I read somewhere that they're hundreds of times more powerful than *our* noses. You know, I've been thinking. Remember how the dogs both fussed and pulled at us when we were on our way home after that guy ran in to us and knocked me down? I mean, he ran right in to the dogs, too, and the leashes got all tangled up, and I'm sure Pookie and Tiger got a good whiff of him. They might be able to tell if they encounter him again. Especially Tiger, after he chased the guy. I think there's some hostility there."

They entered the house, hearing voices from the back as Viola and Gram worked together at something. Moses and Rebel didn't immediately join them to be put back to work, but they paused in the big wide hallway that was almost a room in itself.

"Anyway," Rebel concluded, "what if the dogs were trying to pull us off course because they knew that guy was still off in the shrubbery, sneaking through people's yards, following us? Finding out where we live?"

"And he was doing that because he knew I'd taken his picture," Moses figured, "and he didn't want us to have it. Because he'd just swiped a candy bar from the deli and knocked down an old lady. It's not a real strong case, Rebel. Nobody would do much of anything to him even if they caught him, for stealing twenty dollars and a candy bar."

"No. But it's a possibility. Better than any other

guesses we have. That wallet isn't normal. Did you notice that?"

"Doesn't have anything in it you'd expect to find in a wallet, except cash. No driver's license, credit cards, student passes, ticket stubs, nothing. Almost everybody carries more than this."

They went on through to the kitchen, where Old Vi was stirring pale blue paint with a stick and Gram was starting a pot roast and vegetables in the Crock-Pot on the counter. The both turned when the kids came in, and Pookie gave a happy welcoming bark while Tiger roused himself from a rug in the corner to wander toward them in greeting, tail slowly wagging.

On impulse, Moses extended the wallet toward the big dog. "This smell familiar? It's been wet, but if the guy's carried it for long it might retain his scent."

Tiger sniffed at it obediently, then whined deep in his throat, looking up at the tall boy as if with reproach, his brown eyes distressed.

"I wish you could talk, buddy," Moses told him seriously. "I don't know how to interpret that whine. Do you whine at this?" He pulled a handkerchief out of his pocket and extended it to the big dog. "Does this do anything for you?"

Tiger once more smelled it carefully, then lifted his head to nudge Moses' hand and wag his tail. He did not whine.

"Right. This one smells like me, and the wallet smells like *him*. So how does that get us any closer to finding out who he is?"

"Mrs. Dolzycki said she he snatched a twenty-dollar bill out of her hand. I wonder if she noticed red ink on it. I mean," Rebel explained for the benefit of the grandmothers who were looking somewhat interested, "that would prove it was the same guy who ran away from their store, right?"

"What are they talking about?" Gram wondered aloud.

Viola shook her head. "We'll go crazy if we try to figure it out. That boy is always making up some wild thing to put in his movies. Enough to give an old lady nightmares."

Rebel ignored those remarks and addressed Moses. "Why don't you call and ask her if she noticed the red ink?"

"Good idea," Moses said, and headed for the telephone in the living room. While he was talking to Mrs. Dolzycki, he took the videotape out of his camera and stuck it in the VCR, turning on the television to view it. "You did, huh? Oh, really? Okay, thanks," he said.

Rebel touched his arm. "Ask her if she remembers what kind of candy bar he stole?"

Moses repeated the question, began to smile in what Rebel would have described as an evil way, and hung up. "Guess what?"

"It was a Mars bar, wasn't it?" Rebel guessed.

"Yep. Just like the wrapper we found in the windbreaker. And she remembers the red ink. So it *is* the same bill he grabbed back after using a *different one* to pay for his candy. So that's the guy who swiped my camera after we took his picture. Let's see what he looked like."

He activated the screen with the remote and they sank down on the couch to watch.

The first part of the tape was kind of interesting, shots of the interior of the house, odd angles up the stairs into darkness, that kind of thing. Moses thumbed it into fast-forward, then slowed it again after it had flashed past the pictures of the dogs and kids playing and old people working in their yards.

The thief ran out of the deli, couldn't stop in time to avoid running in to the old lady out front, and left her sprawled among her groceries, heading straight for Moses, Rebel, and their charges. Within seconds the picture went out of kilter, got a view of treetops, then swung across Rebel sprawled on the ground as the legs of the mystery man took off and the dogs milled together, nearly strangling each other with their tangled leashes.

"It went by too fast," Rebel said, leaning forward. "Run it again so we can get a better look at him."

Under Moses' thumb, the film rewound, then began the replay for the second time. When the figure appeared, he stopped it, then inched it forward frame by frame. At first it was disappointing; the fellow was running straight at them but looking down, so that his face was not sharply caught by the camera. And then, just before they crashed, he looked up and straight into the lens.

Moses paused it, and they both leaned close to the TV.

It was a white, almost featureless face. Darkish hair, a little on the long side but not unusual for a college student. Dark eyes, too, and a sharply cleft chin, almost as if someone had made a thumbprint in it. Other than that, he could have been any of hundreds of young men who walked the streets in the U District every day.

Rebel memorized the countenance as best she could. She wished there were some sharply distinctive mole or shape to his mouth or nose, but there was nothing to make positive identity any easier. Only the dent in his chin.

"Find the close-up of his legs and feet when he was heading away from us. Does it show his shoes?" Rebel asked, and waited the few seconds for those to appear on screen.

"Athletic shoes," Moses observed, "and my guess is they're size twelve. See, there, I got a glimpse of my own feet. Much larger."

"Twelve's bigger than most, though. We can eliminate any feet we see that are much smaller. White shoes with turquoise slashes on the sides. We could spot those if they got near us again."

"Yeah, but there are lots of them. Everybody wears athletic shoes, even my dentist. Says they're comfortable to work in. I think it's interesting what Mrs. Dolzycki said about the twenty-dollar bill."

Rebel waited until he'd backed up the tape to take another look. "What, except for the ink stain?"

"Well, she had that bill in her hand, just putting it into the cash register. She had taken it from Mrs. Snelling. When the thief decided he didn't want to pay, after all, he grabbed the twenty out of her hand and took off with it."

Moses waited for her to recognize the significance of that.

"So it wasn't the same twenty he'd used originally to pay for the candy bar," Rebel repeated slowly. "It was a different one."

"And what do we deduce from that?"

"Maybe he thought it was, until he got somewhere he could look at it, and saw the red ink. He'd have noticed if his own bill had ink on it."

"And the reason that might matter is . . . ?"

Rebel had an uneasy feeling that his imagination was working faster than her own. She wasn't used to that. It probably came from the fact that he was used to making up stories to film, and she tried to flag her brain into working faster.

"There was a reason he didn't want to leave her with that original bill, and he only remembered it after he'd given it to her. So there was something about it he didn't want traced back to him. Moses, let me look at those bills again."

Without hesitation, he picked up the wallet from where he'd left it soaking into a newspaper on the floor, and pried out the soggy money.

Rebel laid the bills out side by side on the newspaper. This was the one the guy had grabbed out of

Mrs. Dolzycki's hand. Did it look exactly like the other four?

"I don't suppose either Gram or Viola brought a magnifying glass with them to fix this place up," Rebel observed after a minute or so of close examination. "I can't see any difference in this, but the only thing that occurs to me for him snatching it back is that he didn't want it to go to the bank with the regular deposit. Because," and this time she announced it before he asked his thought-provoking question that might have been designed to show her own ineptitude in figuring it out, "maybe it wasn't a legitimate twenty-dollar bill."

Moses was getting off the floor, having paused the video film. "I just happen to have a magnifying glass in my backpack. No telling when one will come in handy." He fetched the black bag from its resting place at the end of the couch and dug into it, producing the desired object.

Together and separately, they examined the money they'd recovered from the lost wallet. Finally Rebel sank back on her heels, sighing. "They all look identical to me. Including the one with the ink on it, which wasn't his."

"I can't tell them apart either. There's one way we might be able to, though. Give me the glass again."

Moses lined up the bills, somewhat overlapping, and held the magnifier over them. Almost immediately he gave a crow of triumph. "Just as I suspected!" he cried in a creditable imitation of the sleuth in some old B mystery movie.

This time Rebel wasn't far behind.

"All but the one with the ink on it is counterfeit," she said, and saw with satisfaction that they'd reached the same conclusion.

She didn't admit that she wasn't sure how he'd figured it out, but a moment later Moses told her.

8

You thought of it too. The counterfeits all have the same serial number, and it's nothing like the one on the ink-stained bill," Moses said, giving her more credit than she deserved for realizing the meaning of the serial numbers.

"He wasn't thinking when he paid for the candy with a counterfeit bill," Rebel reasoned, "and then when he suddenly realized he'd given it to her, he snatched it back so it wouldn't go to the bank, where somebody would have recognized it as a fake. And why did that matter to him? I mean, he had the money. He must have intended to palm it off on somebody. Why not the Dolzyckis?"

"Well, it wasn't because they knew him, but they might have remembered who gave it to them. What he looked like, if not his name. He didn't want to be traced, obviously. These are pretty good quality, you know. They sure look like the real thing, even if they're counterfeit."

The two grandmothers appeared in the doorway and paused, listening to them.

"What are you kids up to now?" Gram demanded.

"Making up stories," Viola said, nodding. "Don't pay any attention to them. It only makes Moses worse if you ask him about any of them. He'll recite you the entire plot. He's been doing it since he was three years old. Always drove his father crazy. We're about ready to paint that front downstairs bedroom. You guys in your painting clothes?"

"Sure. Be there in a minute," Moses assured them. He stayed where he was, on his knees, looking at the money. "You know what this means, don't you?" That was directed at Rebel.

"That we're in possession of counterfeit money. That's illegal, isn't it? Even if we don't try to spend it? But Mrs. Dolzycki's entitled to her twenty back. The good one."

"And we're going to have to tell the police. I'm going to have to call Uncle Glen. And then I suppose they'll find the guy and lock him up."

"We don't have to tell your uncle right this minute, do we? I mean, we aren't doing any harm by waiting just a little bit," Rebel wheedled. "Seeing what else we can figure out before the cops take everything away from us."

Moses considered, torn between doing what common sense dictated and an unwillingness to give it all up so soon, just when they were beginning to get somewhere.

"He won't like it if we delay very long. Neither," he added, "will my father. He has a very strict viewpoint

on the order of things. That's why we've been in con-
flict practically since I was born. Uncle Glen isn't as
rigid as Dad, but he'd expect me to turn these in as
soon as I realized they weren't genuine."

"Tomorrow?" Rebel suggested hopefully, reluctant
to relinquish the closest thing she'd ever had to a mystery.

"Tomorrow at the latest," Moses agreed, and she
could tell his reluctance matched her own.

"Hey! Moses, come carry this ladder!" Viola
shouted from the next room.

They got to their feet, Moses putting the fraudu-
lent bills back into the wallet and leaving it open,
under the edge of the couch, to dry out. "Coming!" he
yelled back, and then hesitated, turning toward the
window overlooking the front porch. "Hey, there's
somebody out there."

"After the jacket?" Rebel demanded, joining him.

Sure enough, there was a young man standing a few
feet away from them, and when Moses crossed quickly
to the front door and opened it, the fellow actually
had his hand on the torn windbreaker.

"Help you?" Moses asked. He and Rebel both gave
him the once-over: five-eight, stocky build, and hair
that not only stood up in spikes created with a styling
gel but was a deep rusty red.

Not, Rebel decided, the guy on the videotape.

She and Moses were blocking the doorway, and
Tiger pushed against their legs from behind, wanting
to investigate too. Rebel dropped a hand to his collar

to restrain him while allowing him to peer between them at the stranger on the porch.

She guessed the guy's age at early twenties. He was in jeans and a black T-shirt with a rampaging Harley on it, scarlet flames indicating its speed. Even though she'd already eliminated him from being their suspect, her gaze dropped to his feet. Athletic shoes, but no turquoise stripe, only black and white. No size twelve.

The young man jerked around when Moses spoke. His hand was actually on the jacket, but he left it as if he'd been scorched. "Ah—yeah, excuse me."

"Your windbreaker?" Moses asked, sounding friendly. "We found it this morning, blew over against the steps during the storm. We hung it up to dry."

For a moment Rebel could have sworn she saw uncertainty in the rather florid face. "Ah, no, it's not mine," he said.

Beside her, pressing against her leg, Rebel felt Tiger's whine beginning deep inside his massive body.

She refrained from exchanging a questioning look with Moses. She knew he was aware of it too. What was the dog indicating? Was he a lie detector, as well as a watchdog willing to pursue a thief?

There was no way of knowing, but even as Rebel tightened her hold on his collar, Tiger lunged forward, sniffing at the stranger, the way dogs often do with newly introduced people. The whine was audible now, but Tiger didn't make any hostile move such as he'd apparently made when he took out after their mysterious intruder.

The stranger jerked back, his face reflecting alarm at the approach of a dog the size of a small pony.

"He doesn't bite," Moses assured the young man, smiling more broadly now. "Unless you try to steal something, of course. Then he'll tear your arm off."

Rebel hauled back on the collar, and Tiger allowed himself to be drawn away. "I guess you wanted something?" she asked.

"Sure. I was, ah, going to ring the bell and ask about the room."

"What room?" Rebel questioned. She'd seen the sign Moses had painted to hang out front, but it wasn't out there on the lawn yet, and Gram hadn't put up the dollar-store sign in the window, either.

"Oh, I heard you were renting rooms." He sounded a bit flustered. "I have to move soon and I'm looking."

"Where'd you hear about it?" Moses asked, pushing Tiger back into the entryway and closing the door in his face so Rebel didn't have to keep hold of him. "Nobody's advertised a room yet. They're not ready."

"I don't know. Somebody mentioned it. You know how it is in the U District—everybody's always looking for rooms or apartments. Word gets around." His smile looked incredibly false to Rebel. "You will have rooms, though, right, even if they're not ready yet? Could I look at them? Or one of them?"

Moses considered. Rebel wanted to prod him to agree. Even without Tiger's modified reaction to him, she was suspicious of this stranger. He'd been altogether too curious about the torn windbreaker. And

WILLO DAVIS ROBERTS

while not apparently reacting as if this young man was the one he'd chased, Tiger, too, had indicated *something* out of the ordinary.

"If you have a room that is satisfactory, I could stop looking," the stranger urged.

"Okay. Sure, come on in. I'll hold Tiger. You can go on back to where Old Vi's working. That'll be the first room to be ready," Moses decided. "I'm Moses Adams," he said, "and this is Rebel Keeling."

As he stepped inside, Tiger was still near enough to investigate again, nosing into the jeans with more force than Moses had expected. Again the whine was perceptible, and Moses apologized. "Sorry. He's rude sometimes. Doing his duty, you know. Protecting us. What did you say your name is?"

"Ah, I didn't say. Rogers, Henry Rogers," he provided, and Rebel, caught in a generally suspicious mood, wondered if it was his real name.

"Moses! Where are you? We need more newspapers and a drop cloth!" Viola called down the hallway.

"Okay. There's a guy here who wants to see a room to rent. Can we bring him on in?"

Viola stuck her head further into the hallway. "Sure. It's not ready, though. Come on through."

Henry Rogers, or whatever his name really was, had hesitated just inside the front door. He glanced around as if evaluating the place, and even stepped over to peer into the living room. Following his gaze, Rebel noticed that the soggy wallet with its counterfeit bills was barely visible under the edge of the flowered couch. Could Rogers see it too? Would he recognize it for what it was?

But he wasn't the one who'd broken into the house and stolen the video camera, she reminded herself. He wasn't the one Tiger had chased through the stormy night, or the dog would have done more than simply whimper on seeing him again. Besides, he definitely wasn't the one Moses had gotten the pictures of. With that bristly red hair, no one could have mistaken him for *that* individual.

Still, there was something about him that quickened Rebel's senses and her distrust.

"Go ahead and my grandmother will show you the room," Moses told the young man. "I have to get a ladder. Tiger, if you don't stop pulling my arm out of its socket, I'm going to lock you in the kitchen."

"He knows there's something wrong with this guy," Rebel said under her breath as the stranger walked away from them. "I think he just made up the part about wanting a room. He got caught touching the jacket, and if we hadn't gone out there as fast as we did, he could easily have picked it off the railing and walked away with it. Or maybe he wanted an excuse to get inside the house. Did you see him looking toward the couch? That wallet wasn't quite out of sight under it."

"He's not the guy on the video," Moses pointed out.

"No, but what'll you bet he's in cahoots with him? If he is, they'd want that wallet back, and he couldn't have known it wasn't still in the jacket pocket. Moses, when he leaves, let's follow him! See where he goes, who he really is."

"In broad daylight? You think he won't notice?"

"If he's really an innocent guy wanting to rent a room, he'll think we're just a couple of kooks. He won't have anything to hide."

"If he is a co-conspirator, remember that printing counterfeit money is a felony. That could make him dangerous."

"He's only one guy. And we're bigger than he is, and there are two of us. Let's give it a try."

"We can't," Moses said practically. "Our grand-mothers are waiting for us to paint a bedroom. They're not going to let us go without an explanation, and I doubt, even as laid-back as they both are, that they'd think following a possible criminal was a sensible thing to do."

She resisted the urge to stamp her foot, the way she did when her brothers were uncooperative or dense. "Are you chicken, Moses? I thought you liked a girl who had some gumption."

"Gumption, yes. Stupidity, no. If you were my sister, my dad would lock you up."

"But you hardly ever agree with your father!" Rebel protested.

"Well, he's locked me in my room a couple of times," Moses said. They'd walked to the kitchen to retrieve the ladder, and he now carried it in the direction of their next workplace.

Rebel stopped, intrigued. "Really? What for? What did you threaten to do?"

"I didn't threaten. I'd already done it, and he didn't like it."

"What?" she demanded, almost forgetting Henry Rogers who was inspecting the bedroom about to be refurbished. "What had you done?"

"Well, one time I had shaved a cat so it looked like a lion. You know, big brush on the end of it's tail, ruff around its neck. It was a gorgeous Persian, and it looked pretty funny for a while. I didn't actually hurt it. We were putting on a circus, and old Willie made a wonderful lion." He hoisted the ladder over his shoulder. "I was only eight. But because I was so much bigger than other kids my age, he acted as if I should have had the common sense of a twelve-year-old."

"And there were other times you got locked in your room? I never got locked in, only *shut* in, and that was for having a temper tantrum because Mom wouldn't let me go on a skating party with my class at school."

"Why wouldn't she let you go? Had you already misbehaved?"

"No, but she said I looked flushed and when she felt my forehead, she insisted on taking my temperature." Rebel sighed, remembering. "It was one hundred and three."

"So strangely enough she made you stay home. Sounds a lot like *my* mom. Here, let's set this up near

WILLO DAVIS ROBERTS

that wall. That's where we're going to start painting, isn't it?"

"This young man wants to rent this room as soon as it's ready," Gram said cheerfully as they entered. "Isn't that nice? But it may take two coats to cover this ugly green, so it'll be at least a few days before it's ready. Now maybe people will believe this house was a practical purchase; we're going to rent all our rooms by the time the fall quarter starts."

Probably not to Henry Rogers, Rebel thought, but didn't say it. He was looking around as if he really meant to rent a room, though. "And I'd have kitchen privileges and any renters could also use the living room? Is it all right if I take at look at those, too?"

"Sure. Rebel, you show him. Moses, would you carry in that other can of paint from the kitchen? What on Earth is the matter with that dog?"

For Tiger, refusing to be left behind on his rug in the kitchen, continued to pester Henry Rogers, smelling of him up close and personal. *He didn't whimper this way with everybody he met*, Rebel thought. He had sniffed at her, but not with such compelling interest when they were introduced.

"He's just friendly," Moses said easily. "Come on, Tiger, I'm going to turn you loose in the backyard for a while. I think Pookie's already out there, isn't he?"

"No, he was sleeping on his rug under the kitchen table when we left there a few minutes ago. Come back as soon as you've shown young Mr. Rogers the rest of the ground floor. You'll have to share the bathroom with whomever has the other downstairs bedrooms," Gram added.

Pookie was indeed under the table. He opened an eye at his visitors, then closed it.

He hadn't even bothered to get up, let alone bark or whimper over the stranger. But he wasn't the one who had chased the previous intruder, Rebel reminded herself. Pookie had no bad memories of this man. Yet.

Now why had she felt it necessary to add that *yet?*

If it were me actually looking for a room, Rebel thought, *I would ask about the lack of a dishwasher. I don't know anybody who wants to wash dishes.*

His interest in the kitchen was minimal. Now he was asking about the common room he could count on sharing.

"We'll show you," Moses said, and Rebel wondered if she should hurry ahead and kick the lost wallet all the way under the couch or leave it alone and see if their visitor reacted to it. As Moses let the still uneasy Tiger out the door onto the porch, she decided the latter course might reveal more than the former.

If Henry Rogers had come here to retrieve both the windbreaker and the wallet on behalf of a friend or colleague, what would he do if he actually saw the damning evidence in plain sight? How desperate was he to recover it?

It was still there, not quite hidden if you looked down at the floor. Instead of moving quickly to kick it out of sight, Rebel held back, watching Henry Rogers. Had he seen it? Was he interested in it?

WILLO DAVIS ROBERTS

She realized that Moses was keeping a close eye on the fellow too.

Rogers was staring right at the spot where the damp wallet had been slid beneath the couch. Was it her imagination or had his breathing quickened?

Moses flashed a glance at Rebel behind the young man's back as Rogers suddenly bent over and retrieved the wallet.

"Looks like somebody dropped this," he said.

Moses reached around him and took it, perfectly calmly. "It was in that jacket we found, sopping wet. We brought it inside to dry out," he said.

Surely Rebel wasn't imagining Rogers's agitation now. He was clenching his hands as if ready to tear the wet leather object back.

"Did you look in it? Any identification?"

"No." Moses didn't mention the counterfeit bills, but Rebel was now positive that Rogers already knew what had been in it. He just had no way of being sure that they had figured out the bills were bogus. Maybe he thought they planned to spend the money themselves.

"Well, hope the owner comes looking for it," he said lamely. "If you leave the jacket hanging out there, maybe he'll see it and come asking about it."

"Maybe," Moses said. "It's not worth much, so maybe he won't bother. Was there anything else you needed to look at? Do you want to leave a deposit?"

"Deposit?" His face went blank.

"On a room," Moses clarified. "We can't promise

to hold a room for you without a deposit. It'll be ready in three or four days at the most."

"Oh. Oh, well, uh, I don't have my checkbook on me. Maybe I'll be back," Rogers said, and fled.

Moses looked after him for a moment before closing the door. "Something fishy about him, all right. He's not our thief—not the original one, anyway—but he was looking for something other than a room. Tiger did react to him, didn't he? Why would he, if he's not the one Tiger chased?"

"Does that counterfeit stuff have any odor? If they're in it together, they both handled it, so they'd both carry part of the same smell. Could Tiger pick up something like that?"

Moses closed and locked the front door, making a *whooshing* sound. "I wouldn't think so. About the money smelling strange, I mean. I don't think there're any chemicals involved in printing money; it's all done on a home computer. I did notice one thing about this guy: He smokes. I could smell the tobacco on him. Couldn't you?"

Chagrined that she'd missed this clue, Rebel nevertheless nodded. "Yes, he's a smoker. Isn't Tiger used to anybody who smokes?"

"Nope. Yeah, ladies, we're coming!" he called when Viola once more appeared down the hallway outside the room waiting to be painted.

It wasn't until hours later, after the bedroom Henry Rogers wasn't going to rent had been turned from a grungy dungeon into a light, pale blue and appealing

WILLO DAVIS ROBERTS

cave, that Rebel picked up the now dry windbreaker from the porch railing and brought it inside for closer inspection. And she spoke quickly to Moses, because she'd discovered another clue.

"Here," she said, extending it toward his face, "smell this."

9

Moses took the proffered jacket and held it to his nose, sniffing deeply. "Even after getting drenched last night, it still has the smell of tobacco on it, doesn't it? And maybe some body odor. Let's try it on Tiger, see what he thinks of it."

That was easily done, since he'd long since scratched to be let back into the kitchen. He lumbered to his feet when they entered, tail wagging expectantly. The aroma of pot roast was even more tantalizing to the dog than it was to the humans, but he allowed himself to be distracted by the windbreaker.

There was no question that the jacket meant something to Tiger. He issued a deep, low growl when it was held to his nose, looking up into Moses' face as if to convey something urgent.

Unfortunately they were unable to decipher what it was.

Moses dropped the jacket over the back of a chair. "Both guys smelled of tobacco. The BO comes through pretty strong too. It would take more than rain to wash it out. But it seems like it would take more than something as common as the smell of a cigarette to make him suspicious of this Rogers guy."

Rebel made a wild guess, off the top of her head. "Maybe these guys are roommates, and our thief borrowed Rogers's jacket, so it still smelled like *him*. Anyway, I'm convinced Rogers is connected to our thief. You think he'll make another attempt to get the jacket or the wallet?"

"He didn't ask about the money that was in it. Of course he knows it's counterfeit, and he can make some more, if he made this. But I suppose you'd want to be kind of careful where you attempted to pass it, in case anybody else caught on that it wasn't any good."

"Maybe," Rebel speculated, "that's why the thief attempted to grab his bill back from Mrs. Dolzycki. For some reason he didn't want *her* to get it, because when it was deposited the bank clerk would realize it was bad, and she'd remember where she got it, and describe him, and the police would catch up with him."

"You'd make a pretty good fiction writer," Moses observed, scratching behind Tiger's ears as the big dog leaned against him. "Does your family get tired of what you guess at, without any evidence at all?"

"They get tired of me not doing what they want or not thinking the way they do," she had to admit. "This is the first time I've been involved in a real mystery, though, so it's different. If we don't have any solid clues, don't we have to make some logical guesses?"

Moses grinned. "Oh, is that what your guesses were? *Logical?*"

She stuck out her tongue at him. Pookie had become jealous of the attention being paid to Tiger, and now nudged at her legs, so it was necessary to pet him, too.

"Well," Moses said, "our friend Rogers has to realize that we took the money out of the wallet. He probably thinks we're going to spend it. He'd rather spend it himself, so I wonder what he'll do next to try to get it back. How could we use it as bait?"

"You want him to break in and look for it? Gram and Viola wouldn't be happy if we just left the front door open for him."

Tiger's tail suddenly swept the windbreaker off the chair onto the floor, nearly covering Pookie. The smaller dog turned his head and tugged at it, sending it under his feet. In the process he had his snout well into the material, but he gave no indication that the smell of tobacco and body odor meant anything to *him*.

Moses looked around, reaching for a sweater of Viola's that was draped over another chair back. Both dogs, first Pookie and then Tiger, wagged their tails when it was presented at close range.

Bemused, Moses regarded both animals. "Does that mean they both recognize Old Vi's odor and like her? Or just that they think we're playing some stupid game and they're supposed to smile?"

"Try the windbreaker again," Rebel said.

WILLO DAVIS ROBERTS

Pookie wagged his tail—part of the game?—but once more Tiger expressed his distress with a deep-throated whine.

"A truly benevolent God would have made dogs so they could talk," Moses said, giving up.

"But he didn't, so we have to figure it out some other way. Maybe after supper. Boy, that roast smells good!"

It was. They ate heartily, all four of them feeling satisfaction with having gotten one guest room completely painted except for the woodwork. They were tired, but not wiped out, so they decided to do it that evening.

When the phone rang, it was Rebel's mother.

"How are you doing, honey? Tired of being Gram's slave yet?"

"No. We got the kitchen painted yellow yesterday and one bedroom painted light blue today. It's looking pretty good," Rebel reported.

"And you're not bored out of your skull? There's still time to go with us. We haven't exchanged your ticket for a later time yet."

"No, I haven't been bored," Rebel said truthfully.

"And you're not homesick?"

"Mom! I'm fourteen years old. I won't get home-sick. I have Gram and Pookie. And of course Viola is here and her grandson."

"Ah, he's just a little older than you are, right?" Mom's voice took on a different quality. While she'd never voiced the opinion that a girl as tall as Rebel would be at a disadvantage when it came to consider dating, Rebel had always known that her mother considered being petite to be equivalent to being feminine and attractive to the opposite sex.

"Yeah, he's fifteen. His name's Moses of all things. I never met a boy named Moses before."

"Neither did I," Mom agreed. "Is he nice?"

"Sure. He's writing the script for a movie he's going to make." She didn't bother to mention that it was intended to be a horror movie.

Mom cleared her throat. "And, ah, is he . . . good-looking?"

"You mean is he tall."

There was a brief hesitation. "Well, is he?"

"Six-six. Brown eyes, brown hair, and he wears glasses." Luckily Moses wasn't around to overhear this conversation. "I didn't ask to check his teeth. Do you think I should?"

"Rebel! Sometimes you're a little too blunt for a young lady."

"And after all Dad's said about how insignificant height is—in either a guy or a girl—you still couldn't wait to pin that down."

"I didn't ask how tall he is, Rebel. You volunteered it. Six-six? Goodness, and he's only fifteen!"

"I get the impression that there are drawbacks to being extra-tall even if you're a guy. He's not a jock, and some of those try to challenge him, pick fights. All his life people have expected him to act older than he was because he was so big for his age. And he has trouble getting clothes that fit. He wears size sixteen shoes."

"Good grief!" her mother said faintly. Rebel sensed that she was balancing the advantages and disadvantages of what she'd always assumed to be a positive attribute. "Well, it sounds as if you're in good hands and not getting into any kind of trouble."

"Mother," Rebel said with exaggerated patience, "it's been months since I got into any kind of trouble. I'm practically grown-up now, remember?"

She managed to conclude the conversation without either telling an outright lie or giving away anything that might have brought her parents hotfooting it over to rescue her.

She'd never before appreciated how much a devious mind could help in handling all kinds of things. No doubt a lot of kids figured that out in dealing with overzealous parents. It was great that they were concerned for her welfare and that they took the time to talk to her about height and being kind and sensitive to other people's problems and the dangers of drugs and drinking. But after they'd established the ground rules, she longed to be cut free to follow them by herself, with some privacy. Just because she'd done some foolhardy things in the past didn't mean that she was going to be foolish again.

When she hung up the phone and started to rejoin the rest of the clan, something caught her eye, half hidden beneath the same table that held the telephone.

She picked it up and snagged Moses on his way back to the blue bedroom with a can of white semi-gloss for the woodwork. "I've got an idea," she said.

He took that quite calmly. "I can't wait to hear."

She held the freshly painted sign out in front of her so they could both read it. ROOMS TO RENT, it said. "Why don't we hang this up and see who comes to look at the rooms?"

"But they're not ready yet. Oh, you think maybe someone other than Henry Rogers might come and case the joint? How would we tell the legitimate roomers from one of a gang of counterfeiters?"

"I don't know for sure, but it might lead to something. If somebody wants to snoop around, to try to get the wallet back and the bogus bills."

"What do you suggest?" Moses put down his paint can and pried up the lid, ready to cover the old brown paint with glistening white enamel. "We tie a string to the wallet, leave the money sticking out of it to attract his attention, and leave it in plain sight and see if he goes for it?"

"I don't know. We'll think of something. What do you think about the sign? The hooks are already on the frame, so it would be easy to put up. I could do it right now, and that would give anybody looking through the neighborhood a chance to come tonight."

"We're going to Uncle Glen tomorrow, remember? Turn it all over to the police."

Rebel shrugged. "But it wouldn't hurt anything to try to smoke somebody out yet this evening, would it?"

"I think you're an optimist, believing one of the guilty parties will show up in the next couple of hours," Moses said, dipping his brush in the paint. "But go ahead. The worst that can happen is we'll have to keep answering the doorbell."

Before he could change his mind, Rebel was out the front door with the sign, on which Moses had done a good job. It looked professional as she attached its hooks to the dangling chain.

She stepped back to admire it and nearly ran into a lady who had stopped to see what she was doing. "Going to rent rooms, are you?" she asked, stating the obvious.

"Yes. They're not quite ready, but within a week the first ones will be open." She looked closely at the woman. Wouldn't it be great if the first nibble was from someone who was mixed up in the counterfeiting? This lady didn't look likely, though. She was in her sixties, at least, with blue-tinted hair, and she was wearing pearls over a pale green sweater outfit.

"To college kids, I suppose," she said.

"That's what Gram has in mind," Rebel told her hopefully.

The lady shook her head. "My sister is looking for a place, but I don't think she'd be able to handle being around the college crowd. Good luck, though."

Oh, well. Rebel left the new sign swinging gently and returned to the house and the white semigloss, which didn't take long at all with four of them working at it.

The doorbell rang while they were cleaning up.

Rebel whisked away to answer it and found a young man standing there carrying a portable laptop computer. "Rooms?" he asked courteously. Though he had an earring and a gold stud at the side of his nose, he was neatly dressed and presentable.

It was impossible not to think *counterfeiter?* And equally impossible to tell. Rebel thought of criminals as bums, but if they were making money, illegally or not, they could look like *anything*.

"Sure. Come on in," she said. "I'll show you the first one that will be ready in a few days."

They had already arranged that Rebel would show the room, or rooms, and that before the prospective renter had departed, Moses would casually join them, with Tiger padding along behind him, and evaluate the individual.

It had occurred to Moses that from now on they should ask for ID from anyone who showed up to look. This seemed a reasonable request in light of the fact that two elderly ladies would be trusting this person in their own home. That way the person would have to provide them with something that would enable them later to track down anyone they suspected was connected to the counterfeiters.

Rebel and Moses had conferred at length over how to bait a trap. They finally decided that they would leave the windbreaker folded on the telephone table in the living room, with the wallet—one bogus twenty still inside it—underneath it. Out of sight, but visible if anyone moved the jacket.

WILLO DAVIS ROBERTS

"We'll have to arrange to leave each person alone, for a few minutes if we can, in the living room. See if they take the bait," Moses said.

"And if they do? Confront them and get it back?"

"Maybe. We can't really ask for ID until they accept a room. I wonder if I hadn't ought to call Uncle Glen yet tonight. Maybe being amateur detectives isn't a good idea after all," Moses said now, showing signs of uncertainty. "If anybody actually gets away with the evidence, he'll raise blisters on my backside."

It seemed an interesting picture. "Will he really?"

"Well, it's more likely he'll blister my ears. But there were a few times when he paddled my behind."

"What for?" Rebel demanded, fascinated. She'd suffered through any number of punishments over her lifetime, but spanking hadn't been employed since she had outgrown her defiance of warnings when she was little more than a toddler.

"Once it was because I set a fire in the trash beside his garage. The other time it was when I was pretending to have an adventure on the high seas and I ran the water over the top of his bathtub and it leaked through into the room below."

"Yech. I think even my dad might have paddled me for either one of those. Why did you start the fire?"

"I wanted to see what would happen. I found out. It was the last fire I ever experimented with until I was old enough to build campfires under adult supervision. What do you think? Are we taking too many risks here after all?"

"What's risky about putting up a sign saying 'Rooms for Rent'? There are four of us here in the house, so we'll outnumber any crook that shows up. And we have two dogs to protect us. Pookie isn't good for much except making a racket, but Tiger's more aggressive than you thought he was. After all, he chased that guy quite a long way and might have caught him if he hadn't gotten all tangled up in that big branch."

Moses inhaled deeply, considered, then nodded. "Okay. Let's go ahead and finish the painting and see if anybody else turns up."

They soon had proof that there was a demand for rental rooms in the U District. By the time the second looker rang the bell, Gram looked around from the woodwork she was painstakingly detailing. "What's going on? Did you kids hang out our shingle already?"

"Sure. Might as well have the place filled as soon as we get ready," Moses said easily. "Why don't you get the door, Rebel, and the rest of us can keep on working?"

"Okay." Rebel wiped a glob of paint off her hand on a rag and headed for the door. Tiger, who had been lying quietly watching the job as if he were the foreman, rose without invitation and moved silently beside her into entryway.

This one was different. Tall enough to look her in the eye, skinny, with hair that was bleached blond on one side and purple on the other side. He had an open, friendly face. "Hi," he said. "I'm here about the room."

WILLO DAVIS ROBERTS

"Come on in," Rebel said, stepping backward and pulling the door open more widely. "The rooms won't be ready for a few days, but we're renting now if people want to hold them."

"Sounds good. I need something kind of cheap," the boy said. Rebel had trouble keeping from staring at the hair. "I can't stand living at home anymore, and everything I've seen so far is too expensive."

"You're a student at U-Dub?"

"Yeah. Premed." That was mind-boggling. She'd never known a doctor with purple hair. Maybe he'd outgrow the need for it by the time he hung out his shingle, if doctors still did that.

"You'll have to talk to my grandma and her friend about the rent," Rebel said. "You'd have kitchen privileges and the use of the living room. We haven't redecorated in here yet, and I think they're going to get some more easy chairs and maybe another couch." She paused just inside the wide archway, allowing this new fellow to see the bait on the telephone table. He didn't seem to pay any attention to it. "You might as well take the tour so you can make up your mind."

His name was Ernie Dodge. "It'd be okay if I played my guitar, right?"

Rebel hesitated at that. "You'd have to ask my grandma. She wouldn't want you to disturb the other roomers."

"Everybody likes my guitar," Ernie assured her with a grin.

Gram openly evaluated his hair colors. "Why on Earth would you want to do that to what was apparently perfectly nice hair?" she asked him without hesitation.

The grin widened. "Because it bugs my old man. Everything about me bugs him, which is why I'm moving out. If this room you're working on will be ready later this week, I'll take it."

"Don't you want to see the rest of the house before you decide?" Rebel asked. "The bathroom? The kitchen?"

"A bathroom's a bathroom. Has all the right equipment, right? And I don't cook anything except in a microwave. Do you have one?"

When assured that they did, he nodded. "Okay. I'll take it."

"You want to put a deposit on it to hold it?" Moses asked from high up on a ladder where he was finishing a molding.

"Uh, is ten dollars enough? That's all the cash I have on me."

"Ten dollars and some ID. We need to verify who you are." Moses didn't explain why that mattered to the landlords. He gave the molding one last slap and started down to the floor.

Rebel examined the driver's license. The face in the picture was the same, but the hair was an ordinary medium brown. She took his money and wrote him a receipt in the book that Gram had ready.

Tiger, while pacing with her to let him out, gave no

indication that he had ever encountered him before or that he objected to him in any way. "Nice dog," Ernie said as he went out.

There were three more visitors before the evening ended. Two girls, giggling over the bathroom, the assurance that there *would* be a dishwasher, and the color the room was before it was to be painted pale green, decided one of them would take that room when it was ready. The girl didn't have either cash or a checkbook, but did have ID, which Rebel quickly memorized. "I'll be back tomorrow with a check," the girl, Lisa Tremont, promised.

The final visitor was also female. Her name was Claudia Hinton, and she was only a couple of inches shorter than Rebel, only, Rebel thought regretfully, with a much shapelier figure in a black short-sleeved pullover, advertising Snohomish Baptist Church on the back of it, and tight black jeans. Claudia could easily have been a model with her perfect, understated makeup and long black hair.

Since the other rooms to be rented next were upstairs, she followed Rebel up there to peer into each of them. She hesitated at Rebel's own quarters. "This one would be nice, but it's already occupied."

"I'm only staying a few weeks, if you want to wait that long. Or I can move into one of the other rooms until I leave for Germany."

"Doing Europe, are you?" Claudia flicked her a smile. "I went last year. Loved Paris and Brussels, especially. Look, I'm not in a big hurry. My rent's paid at my present place until the end of the month. Why don't I put money down on this one?"

"Fine," Rebel said, and wrote out the receipt.

She did her act of allowing the girl to check out the living room while she responded to a summons from Moses and left her alone for a few moments. Patiently, Tiger stood guard while Rebel was gone, making not a sound.

She returned to find Claudia in the entryway, smiling her thanks. "See you in a week or so, and you can let me know when that room will be ready."

Moses joined Rebel a moment after Claudia left, munching on a sandwich that oozed peanut butter and jelly. "Well, that was a bust, wasn't it? We've got the rooms half rented already, though."

"Nobody seemed interested in the windbreaker or the wallet at all," Rebel said, disappointed.

Yet when they moved into the living room, after Claudia had walked down the front steps, the torn jacket and the wallet with its counterfeit bill, which Rebel could have sworn were still on the table, had vanished.

10

M oses clenched his fists until his knuckles turned white.

Rebel felt as if she'd been slugged in the gut. She'd experienced that one time when her brother Wally had hit a line drive right into her stomach, and the sensation was pretty much the same.

"Uncle Glen is going to kill me," Moses said in a voice an octave lower than normal.

"If my folks hear about this, they'll hold a double funeral," Rebel muttered. "How could anybody have gotten the stuff out of here? Nobody was left alone with it for more than a minute or so, and I let them all out. Claudia was the last one in here, and she'd moved from the living room out into the hall when I wasn't watching her, but she couldn't have hidden that jacket on her person. None of them was carrying a backpack or a bag that jacket would have fitted into. It would have showed if they'd stuffed it under their clothes. Tiger was alongside the whole time, too. He's reacted every time he got close to the jacket. Surely he would have detected it if someone tried to walk out with it."

"But the jacket and the wallet with the bill in it are gone." Moses grimaced as he pushed with the heels of his hands against both sides of his head. "How?" He squeezed, as if by so doing he could force some logic into his brain. "How am I going to explain that we had evidence and let it slip through our fingers? There might have been fingerprints on the money, though we've still got the other bills. But they might have been able to trace the jacket, even if it was old. The state forensic lab can come up with all kinds of information from something like that. Oh, why didn't we just call the cops in the first place?"

"Don't panic," Rebel advised, though her heart was pounding too. "It wasn't a bad idea. It just didn't work out quite the way we hoped."

"Boy, that's an understatement!" Moses audibly ground his teeth. "The question is, what are we going to do now? Call the police and admit how stupid we've been? Take our verbal whipping and—" An expression of further dismay twisted his face. "You don't think they'll do anything more than bawl us out, do you? We used bad judgment, but we didn't do anything *criminal*, did we?"

"Nobody's going to put us in jail for it," Rebel said firmly, though she wasn't absolutely certain of that. She'd learned from experience that showing confidence often won the day when going wishy-washy just got you walked on. "Look, it's already too late to call your uncle or someone else on the police force *before* anything happened, so right now we have to use our own brains and solve this mystery. *Then* we can present it to the police to do whatever's necessary about arresting the criminals."

Moses didn't look any happier. "They're still going to be totally furious with us."

Rebel hoped all of this wouldn't break until her parents had gone abroad. They'd have to be told, of course—maybe Gram could be talked into explaining to them what had happened, so she wouldn't have to do it herself—but by the time they came home, or she joined them for the grand camping tour, they'd have had time to cool down a little.

"There's no point in worrying about things we can't help. Let's concentrate on what we *can* do: *solving* this thing."

"And you've got an idea how to do that?" He was looking at her the way her brothers sometimes did when she proposed something they considered to be off-the-wall.

"Well, let's apply logic," Rebel said, retaining her ill-founded attitude of confidence. "We know we put the jacket over the top of the wallet and left them on the phone table, right? We hoped that if any of the criminals showed up, they'd notice and give themselves away."

"Somebody noticed, all right, and managed to beat us at our own game," Moses said morosely.

"Agreed. But our idea of hanging out the sign to give them a chance to get into the house worked." She thought that giving him part of the credit for that was practical, even though it had actually been her own idea. "People came almost as soon as we hung it out there."

"They came, they saw, they stole," Moses pointed out.

"But we know it was one of the people who came," Rebel reminded him. "So that narrows the field, doesn't it? We know they're watching us, looking for a way to get their property back. They were brazen enough to break in to the house in the first place—well, they took advantage of the fact that the door was left unlocked and came inside and stole your video camera because you got a picture of the guy who passed the counterfeit bill and then tried to snatch it back—and then one of that guy's friends came back here under the pretense of wanting a room in order to recover the evidence before we could turn it over to the police."

One of her brother Wally's favorite expressions when talking to her was, "Are you giving me a snow job again, Rebel?" Usually she was. If she inundated him with words, it confused him. At any rate it seemed to be having a calming affect on Moses.

"They can't know we haven't already done that."

"They know no cop has shown up on their doorstep yet to arrest them. So they have to take the chance they can still keep that from happening. Printing money is a felony, so they're going to try hard to stay out of prison."

"Okay. Granted. But if they now have the evidence, where do we go from here?"

"This is where using our brains comes in. We figure out what happened to the jacket and the wallet and the money."

After a moment when he contemplated her with a visible lack of conviction, Moses cleared his throat. "Okay. What is *your* brain coming up with?"

"I don't see how any of those people who were here today could have carried the jacket and the wallet out of here without being detected. It was too bulky to hide considering they were all wearing summer clothes and not carrying anything they could have concealed it in."

"So?" Moses prompted when she stopped.

"So they didn't get it," Rebel said, suddenly gloriously enlightened. "It's all still here!"

He looked around the room, which was so sparsely furnished that everything seemed to be in plain sight right now, except for some newspapers scattered on the floor in preparation for the next work to be done here. None of them was deep enough to cover anything as thick as the jacket.

"You're the detective," he conceded, leaving the ball in her court, so to speak.

"None of our visitors was alone in this room for more than a matter of seconds," Rebel reasoned. "So it had to have been hidden somewhere close by, so they could come back and get it later."

Their gazes swept the telephone table—no place for concealment there—and the old flowered couch and the three comfortable if mismatching chairs—in frustration.

"Could anyone besides the last one, what's her name, Claudia, have taken the stuff? Are you absolutely positive it was still there when you left her alone for that minute or two?" Moses demanded.

Rebel wanted to insist that she was certain, but truthfully she had to hesitate. Could it have been moved before that? She *thought* she'd checked every time a different person was in the room, but maybe she'd missed. She gnawed on her lower lip, then shrugged. "I guess anything's possible. I sure thought I was keeping a close eye on it."

The arched doorway was wide, showing them the entryway, which was completely unfurnished. And— Rebel drew in a hopeful breath, estimating how far a thief could go in such a short time—the door under the stairway where someone had added a closet. It had been empty when they arrived, because she'd looked when she was taking the tour.

She stepped quickly into the entry and jerked open the closet door.

Even then she might have missed it if she hadn't had such a strong motivation for poking into the back corner, the darkest part. It was almost invisible there, the dark blue jacket. And sure enough, the wallet was still there, too, one counterfeit twenty-dollar bill still in it.

She gave a triumphant cry and pulled them out to hand them over to Moses.

"See? When one thing's impossible, you have to figure out what's *possible*."

Moses looked as if he'd just been acquitted of a major offense. "So they're coming back. When? Who?"

"Which one of them was it? The one who had the most time to maneuver was that last one, the model-type lady Claudia Hinton. She doesn't seem a likely candidate, though."

"Why not? Girls—women—commit crimes too. Wonder if she left fingerprints on the wallet when she handled it, or if she picked it up with the jacket. It's smooth leather; I think it would hold prints."

"And when I wrote a receipt for her down payment," Rebel said with satisfaction, "I wrote her driver's license information on it. I was sure she would object to that, but she didn't say anything."

"Probably figured she'd be back and retrieve the stuff before we figured out what would happen. Bold as she was, she might even have come back and actually rented the room for a month or so. On the other hand, if they've printed out lots of money, there might be enough to allow her to disappear to somewhere else before we figured out what happened."

He inhaled, exhaled, then deferred to her. "Okay, Sherlock, what do we do next?"

"Next," Rebel said with fully restored confidence, "we set a trap."

Before he could ask her how, she hoped to think of something.

Moses took off his glasses and swiped a hand across his mouth. He wasn't smiling. "There's only one thing to do," he said. "Call the police."

"But we're so close to solving this!" Rebel protested. "How can we give up now?"

He regarded her as if she'd suddenly grown an extra eye in the middle of her forehead. "How can we not? We're in over our heads. These guys could be dangerous. I don't know what the sentence is for someone convicted of counterfeiting, but I'm pretty sure it would be years in prison. They aren't going to take that lying down if they can help it, and we're in their way."

"I never figured you for chicken," Rebel said, bitterly disappointed.

He was not disconcerted. "I've lived with a lawyer all my life. I didn't want to follow in his footsteps, but I heard what he said every night at the dinner table. And one of the things he repeated was that people got into trouble by being stupid, and that included not calling in the cops when it was appropriate. Rebel, face it. *Now* is appropriate."

Her usually agile mind had not yet come up with a viable solution that she could offer to him in its entirety. And in the very back of it was the recognition that her parents would agree with Mr. Adams: It was time to call 911.

That wasn't quite what Moses had in mind. "No, they're all strangers and they'll treat us like idiots. Uncle Glen will be ticked off, but he knows me. He'll believe me. I'll call him at home."

Dejectedly, Rebel sank onto the end of the couch while he dialed his uncle's home number.

"Uh, hi, Aunt Dee? Moses. Could I speak to Uncle Glen, please?"

There was a brief silence. Rebel watched dismay creep over Moses' face before he said, "You mean he won't be back until *tomorrow?*" Another silence. "Well, no, it's not exactly an emergency, but . . . it's important. Would you tell him I need to talk to him as soon as possible? And uh, I'm not at home. I'm at the house Old Vi bought with her friend, Mrs. Keeling. He knows where it is. I think she even gave him a key. Um, urgent? Well, kind of. Yes, it's personal. Okay, thanks, Aunt Dee."

He hung up the phone as if he were reluctant to let go of it. "You heard. He's gone fishing. *Fishing!* Right when I really need him. He'll be back either late tonight or by noon tomorrow. He goes on duty again tomorrow night." His grimace expressed his frustration. "I always thought if I ever got in trouble, I could count on Uncle Glen. He bawls me out when I get off base, but he's a lot more human than my father. He'll at least hear the whole story before he throws me in jail or puts me on restriction for the rest of my life." In torment, he demanded, "Do your folks ever put you on restriction? No TV, no computer, no phone, no anything? For months and months?"

"Once in a while," Rebel admitted cautiously. "Not for months. Maybe for two weeks. That was the longest I ever got."

"What for?"

"It doesn't matter," she evaded, remembering only too well how angry her mother had been because she'd stayed in the theater past her curfew to watch an exceptional film for a second time through. "Well, we're down to two choices, aren't we? Either wait until your uncle comes home, or talk to a policeman who's a stranger and who will shine a light in our faces and grill us until we break."

"It's not funny," Moses rebuked her, putting his glasses back on. "What if Uncle Glen doesn't come before the counterfeiters show up? How can we be prepared for whatever they'll try to do? They didn't get the jacket and the wallet and the bogus money out of the house yet, but they'll try, as soon as possible. Probably even tonight."

Tiger, hearing the serious discussion and no doubt interpreting enough of Moses' tone to realize he was distressed, pushed against Rebel's knee as if to help.

She scratched absently behind his ear, which while she was sitting down was at a level with her own face.

"Tiger will protect us. Won't you, boy?" she murmured, and the Irish wolfhound wagged his tail, reassured.

"Oh, sure. If they come with guns blazing, he'll be a whole lot of help."

"If they were going to come with guns blazing, they'd have done it by now. They're still trying to salvage their operation, whatever it involves. Counterfeiting is a sort of nonviolent crime, isn't it?"

"How do I know? I've never been mixed up with criminals before, not up close and personal. Seems to me that thinking about being sentenced to twenty years in prison might make them violent now, if they haven't been before. People are always thinking that just because I'm bigger than everybody else I must be stronger, braver, smarter, whatever. It's not fair. I'm just an ordinary guy, Rebel. I don't know how to deal with something like this!"

"Aren't you kids going to help us clean up?" Gram called from the kitchen door down the hallway. "We thought we'd microwave some popcorn when we get everything lined up so we can start fresh tomorrow morning."

For once Moses was not intrigued by the thought of food, though he squared his shoulders and straightened up to his full six feet six. "Come on," he told Rebel, "let's go do it. If anybody shows up before Uncle Glen does, we call 911 immediately, agreed?"

For once Rebel didn't have an alternate suggestion. She didn't know how to deal with desperate criminals either. She stood up and, still fondling Tiger's ear, followed him back to the kitchen.

Painting wasn't so bad, because you could see that you'd accomplished something and it looked great. Cleaning up was a bit of a drag, though. Rollers and brushes had to be cleaned; sticky, stained tarps and newspapers had to be disposed of. Lids on partial cans of paint remaining had to be tamped on securely, and in spite of his denials, Moses' strength came in handy for that and lifting things too heavy for Rebel and the old ladies.

Anything they weren't going to use again was stuffed into one of the big garbage cans on the back porch to be hauled away later. The paint cans still to be used were stacked in a group on the kitchen floor. There were too many empty ones to fit in the trash cans so they were piled alongside them.

Viola looked critically at her morose grandson when they settled around the table with their bowls of popcorn. "What's wrong with you, Moses?"

"Nothing special," he denied. "Just wrestling with a . . . problem."

Viola nodded and explained to Gram, "He's been moody like this since he was a little boy. He was always making up stories, working out plots, thinking like the genius he is. I remember one time he got so involved in a stage set he was building out of cereal boxes and those round oatmeal containers that he didn't leave in time for the bathroom and he wet his pants."

"Vi! Holy cow, what a thing to tell them!" Moses said, flushing. "Just because you're my grandma and know a lot of my secrets, you don't have to spill them all to just anybody!"

"We're not just anybody," Gram said, reaching out to pat one of his big hands where he'd clenched it on the table. "We're family, Moses. All of us have that kind of mishap in our pasts. Why, I could tell you one about Rebel when she was about seven—"

"Gram! Hush! He's not interested in what any stupid seven-year-old kid did," Rebel interrupted, nudging her grandmother firmly under the table.

Luckily Moses was sufficiently engaged in worrying about what to do if the counterfeiters showed up before his uncle did that he didn't push the issue. He ate his popcorn, though it was obvious his heart wasn't in it. Once in a while somebody dropped a kernel or two on the floor for the expectant dogs.

At a quarter to ten, as they were stacking their bowls in the sink to be added to the breakfast dishes, the phone rang.

"Get that, will you, Moses?" Viola requested.

Expectantly, Rebel trailed along after him, in case it might be something that called for her own input.

It was Uncle Glen's wife, Dee. She'd just had a phone call from her husband saying that he'd be getting in after midnight. Did Moses want him to come over that late or wait until morning?

Turning his shoulder against Rebel's attempt to advise him, Moses said firmly, "Yeah, tell him to come even if it's late. I'll wait up for him. Thanks."

When he'd hung up, Rebel asked quietly, "Do you want me to wait with you, or would you rather be by yourself?"

"No, why would I want to be by myself? Unless those guys come at the front door with a battering ram, it's going to be pretty boring sitting here alone. In the dark. Or do you think I should leave the lights on?"

"You mean, do we want to scare them off with lights or make them think it's safe to try to break in if it's dark?"

"Yeah. Which? Personally, I'd just as soon they didn't try anything before Uncle Glen gets here. I don't suppose you're packing a gun, are you?"

His attempt at humor suggested he was also attempting to cope with possibilities.

"Nope. Forgot my six-shooter this time out. Let's leave the lights on here in the living room until midnight, anyway. Then if your uncle doesn't show up by then we'll turn them off and they'll think we've gone to bed."

"Thereby issuing them an invitation to break in. How many places are there they could do that? Front door, back door, and windows all around the lower floor would be within reach if they either brought a ladder or boosted one guy up on another one's shoulders. Maybe we should make the rounds and make sure all the windows *are* locked."

"Or that one is 'accidentally' left unlocked. If they get in and go directly to the closet, we'll know for sure we have the right people cornered."

"Cornered, right! And they will just stand there doing nothing while we tie them up until the cops get here. Can you dial 911 in the dark?"

"Sure," Rebel guaranteed.

"Are we going to leave the jacket and wallet where we found it? In the back corner of the closet?"

"Why don't we put something else there that will feel the same if they look for it in the dark and keep the real evidence somewhere else. Just in case they get away from us."

"Oh, you're no longer convinced they'll submit readily to being tied up?" He gave her a sardonic grin. "Maybe there's still hope for you. I've got a black T-shirt upstairs that would seem about the same if they didn't have the light on. I'll go get it. We need something to mimic the weight of the wallet wrapped in it, too. I hope they're in enough of a hurry, if they come, not to waste time examining it too closely."

"I'll produce the wallet," Rebel offered, and he went up to the attic for the dark shirt. After they inspected it, though, they decided that the texture of it wouldn't fool anybody who'd ever handled the real jacket. They searched through the garments hanging in the rear hall and hoped that a substitute could be made of a ragged windbreaker someone had left there.

Rebel handed over the packet, fashioned of tightly folded newspapers, and demonstrated how it felt through the cloth of the jacket. "It's the right size, feels pretty close."

"Okay. Let's hide the real evidence under one of the sofa cushions. It'll be easy to get at there when Uncle Glen gets here." He sighed. "I hope he remembers what it was like to be a stupid kid. He must—Old Vi tells stories on him. She even tells tales on my dad. It's hard to believe some of them, because Dad doesn't act as if he ever did anything less than perfect. He sure doesn't expect any of his sons to be young and foolish."

"It isn't as if you deliberately went looking for trouble," Rebel pointed out. "We were just walking the dogs, and you took this guy's picture because he was running straight at you."

"Logic—*my* logic—never makes an impression on my father."

Rebel was beginning to believe that her own dad seemed great by comparison with Mr. Adams. She hoped that he still would after he heard about all of this.

Uncle Glen had not come by midnight. They turned off the lights and waited in the darkness, their nerves increasingly on edge.

The conspirators showed up twenty minutes later.

There were only three of them, but Moses and Rebel didn't know that.

It sounded to them as if they were being invaded by entire hordes of Pharaoh's armies.

When the glass smashed in the darkened dining room, Tiger woke from his sleeping position on one of Rebel's feet and for the first time they heard him bark.

Afterward, both of them admitted it had been awesome. Deep, powerful, fearsomely raising the hairs on the backs of their necks.

Pookie chimed in only a moment later, obviously smaller in sound and stature but just as incensed at this intrusion.

"Call 911!" Moses said, and leaped across the room for a light switch.

So she didn't have to call in the dark after all. Rebel had always imagined how competently she would have dialed that number in an emergency, and this sure qualified.

A calm voice asked, "What is your emergency, please?"

"Someone breaking into our house! Hurry. They've smashed a window! There's a gang of them!" She gave the address, amazed that at the moment of stress, with her pounding heart almost drowning out the voice on the phone, she actually remembered what the street number was, when it wasn't even her own house.

Through the archway she saw and heard the action as three young male figures exploded from the vacant dining room, directly across the hall from the closet where they assumed their objective to be hidden.

Rebel had thought she was prepared, but when it actually happened, it was scarier than she'd expected.

"What do you want?" Moses asked loudly, and as far as Rebel could tell, quite calmly. He'd grabbed Tiger by the collar and now held him with an effort, because the big dog was lunging forward, trying to reach the intruders.

The first thing that registered about them was that all three had pulled nylons over their heads to disguise their features, and they all wore plain dark T-shirts and ordinary jeans.

The second thing was that they weren't apparently armed; they had no weapon except, as they supposed, surprise. No doubt they thought the inhabitants of the house would have to come from upstairs or the rear bedrooms and wouldn't reach the ground floor until they'd escaped with what they came for. That wasn't particularly reassuring, however, because she and Moses were still outnumbered and neither of them had any training in holding off an assault.

Not even with the help of an Irish wolfhound who was growling and barking and showing some very formidable teeth.

The intruders stopped, only a dozen feet away from Moses and the dog.

"Hold him off and nobody needs to get hurt," one of them said.

"The cops are on the way," Moses informed them, sounding barely different from his normal, confident self. "You'd better leave."

"Not likely," the tallest of the trio stated, "until we get what we came for. Get out of the way."

"What did you come for?" Moses asked, as if innocently. He told Rebel later that at that point he started praying his uncle would show up late, but not *too* late to be of help.

"Just let us get it and we'll be out of here," the third one said, and made a tentative movement toward the closet under the stairs.

Tiger was truly furious by now, and there was a question as to whether Moses had the strength to hold him. And then, as their enemy jerked open the door of the closet and bent to reach inside, Moses either let him free or the dog won out.

Tiger wasn't bluffing, either. As the young man grabbed the bundle Rebel and Moses had substituted for what he was really after, the dog nailed him. Right in the posterior still protruding at a handy level for the dog to bite by lowering his head only a little.

The guy screamed and withdrew from the closet, with Tiger still maintaining a pretty good hold.

"Don't drop it!" the tall one yelled. "Come on, let's get out of here!"

At that point a key scrabbled in the front lock and a big man burst through the front door right behind Moses. Uncle Glen, six feet five as billed, only much heavier through the shoulders and chest than Moses was.

"What in blazes is going on?" he demanded as the trio of interlopers fled toward the back of the house.

"Counterfeiters, we've got the evidence," Moses said, jogging after them. Tiger was still giving them a bad time and he didn't want the dog to be hurt.

Gram and Viola both popped out of their bedrooms near the back end of the hallway at about the same time, bewildered and anxious. "What's going on?" Gram demanded, but nobody had time to reply.

Rebel still held the phone in her hand, blocking out whatever the 911 dispatcher was saying, and Uncle Glen spoke to her sharply as he followed Moses and the intruders deeper into the house. "Tell dispatch officer needs assistance at this address!"

That was the quickest way to get a police response, he told them later. Only "officer down" works any faster, and luckily this officer was not down.

Rebel relayed that message, was told to stay on the line until help arrived, and had to be content with Moses' version of events after the mob disappeared into the kitchen. There was a lot of yelling, Uncle Glen's authoritative tones commanding someone to "freeze," and then a crashing that Rebel figured meant someone had run into the pile of paint cans beside the back door.

Moments later the fleeing counterfeiters encountered the garbage cans and empty paint containers on the back porch, and there was more yelling.

Through it all, Tiger proved he was worthy of his name. He stopped barking, but he held on until a chunk of bloody jeans came off in his mouth, then dropped that to make another attack on flesh.

The police car arrived at the curb moments later, lights flashing, siren cutting the night in a way to bring neighbors out of their beds to peer through windows in astonishment. A second patrol car was right behind it, and when two uniformed officers pounded up the steps, Rebel gestured and called out. "Go around back!" she said, and they obediently swerved to run around the house toward the gate at the side. As soon as they'd passed, she said, "They're here," to the dispatcher and hung up the phone.

She was missing out on all the good parts. If she and Moses were both going to be in trouble for not calling in the cops any sooner, at least she wanted to be in on the finish.

The kitchen was a disaster area.

Paint cans had been scattered across the linoleum that now would probably have to be replaced after all. In spite of Moses' attempts to reseal them, several lids had come off and rolled away from their containers to allow the contents to spill out in still-widening yellow and blue and pink puddles. It might have been pretty, but it wasn't, with them all running slowly together that way.

One of the invaders had escaped through the back door and was trying to disentangle himself from the trash cans on the porch while Tiger continued to bite whatever part he could reach. Rebel guessed—correctly, as it later transpired—that this was the one whose smell had been familiar because Tiger had chased him before.

Uncle Glen—wearing an old fishing hat and a plaid shirt with jeans rather than a police uniform—had slammed another of the fellows against the freshly painted yellow wall, where his hands left a bloody smear as they slid upward. Evidently he, too, had encountered Tiger's canines at some point.

Rebel winced, hoping the stains would wipe off and that they wouldn't have to repaint that wall. Gram and Viola were going to be appalled. So far the old ladies hadn't ventured into the kitchen to determine what horror was in progress, preferring to wait where they were until things calmed down.

The third interloper was nowhere in sight, but at about the same time that Rebel reached the point where she could observe, she heard additional voices raised as the other two officers encountered that one as he tried to get through the gate toward the street.

With his prisoner under control and fellow officers

taking care of the ones who'd made it outside, Uncle Glen surveyed Moses with what appeared to be moderate displeasure. "You want to tell me what's been going on? Dee said you needed to talk to me, but I didn't figure you were under attack by a gang."

Moses licked his lips, nervous now that he was face-to-face with authority, even if it was in the form of his favorite uncle. "Well, it's going to be kind of a long story. See, we sort of stumbled on to these counterfeiters, I took one's picture by accident and—"

Uncle Glen reached over and jerked the concealing nylon mask over his victim's head, not gently. "How'd you know it was this one, with his face covered up?"

"Not this one, the one Tiger's chewing on," Moses said. "I'm pretty sure."

It was Rebel who verified that, indicating the ruined floor covering. "We saw his footprints in two different places, and there they are again, in yellow paint. It's a pretty distinctive pattern on his soles. Moses made a sketch of them when we first saw them."

Uncle Glen's gaze sharpened. "And how long ago was this? You a detective now?"

"Well, we didn't have any real evidence to begin with, just suspicions, and by the time things started to jell, I *did* call, and you'd gone fishing."

Somehow that didn't seem to pacify the big man who still hovered over the suspect with the bloody handprints upraised against the wall. He scowled at Moses while he spoke to that one. "Put your hands down, behind your back."

Even on a fishing trip, it seemed, he had been prepared with those plastic handcuff things. It didn't appear to bother him that the young man was bleeding.

"Who was your getaway car driver?" he asked the youth.

A contorted face twisted toward them as he replied. "I don't know what you're talking about."

"Okay. We'll ask you again down at the station. Girl driving, a '90 Subaru, light gray, motor running when I pulled in behind her. She took off like a scalded cat, but not before I got her license number. Soon as we get this group wrapped up, I'll call it in and they'll pick her up before she goes very far."

Rebel hesitated, then offered, "She might have been one of the girls who came here pretending she wanted to rent a room. We got ID on them so we might help you find her faster if she goes home."

Uncle Glen had a very firm jaw. "I think this is going to be an interesting explanation, when we get around to it." The impression they got was that the amateur detectives were in for as blistering a time as the criminals. When Rebel exchanged a glance with Moses, she could tell that he had the same expectations.

One of the uniformed officers stepped into the back doorway, holding up the bundle they'd used to fake out the intruders. "One of 'em was clutching this for dear life, then threw it away when I grabbed him. Looks like an old jacket shirt and a bundle of newspapers wrapped in masking tape."

WILLO DAVIS ROBERTS

Now it was Rebel's turn to clear her throat. "The jacket was hanging in the hall. I made up the packet so they'd think they had the wallet with the counterfeit money in it."

By this time Uncle Glen was glowering. "I thought I taught you a long time ago, if you need a cop, call one."

"You were fishing," Moses said feebly, eliciting a brusque response rejecting this on the spot.

"I'm not the only cop in Seattle. Your old man is going to have a few words with you on the subject too, before we're through, I suspect."

"Are you going to have to tell Dad?" Moses' voice held little hope of a miracle.

"From what I've gathered so far, with none of the details, it strikes me that this is going to wind up on the front page of the papers and on TV news." Uncle Glen crushed his hopes. "You and your friend," he glanced at Rebel, "are going to have to go into court and testify to whatever happened. These guys will probably be arraigned in the next day or two, and you'll be subpoenaed for that and the trial. Both of you. Maybe Ma and her friend."

It took Rebel a moment to discern that "Ma" was Viola.

Another problem instantly arose. "I'm supposed to join my family in Europe in a couple of weeks. It won't take longer than that, will it?" she asked.

He gave her a keen glance that made her glad she wasn't one of the primary culprits in this mess. "I suggest you forget about going to Europe anytime soon. The judge will probably order you not to leave town until it's all been resolved. Testifying at the arraignment, before a grand jury, in a courtroom trial, however it comes out."

"But my folks are going on a caravan trip there for several weeks!" Though Rebel didn't intend to sound pathetic, she couldn't quite keep the distress out of her voice.

For the first time Uncle Glen's mouth softened with a touch of humor. "Sorry, honey, but I'm afraid you're going to miss it. Come on, sergeant, let's get this crew on their way to jail. Have somebody seal up that broken window. I want to get some sleep yet tonight, so why don't you give me a rundown on all of this, Moses. Ma, maybe you could put on a pot of coffee."

Viola and Gram had haphazardly dressed and emerged into the brightly lighted kitchen, as eager as Uncle Glen to hear the explanations that would be forthcoming. Gram winced as she stared at the reddish streaks on her formerly pristine yellow wall.

The officers used no sirens or lights when leaving. Rebel sort of wished Uncle Glen would leave his part of the investigation until morning so that she, too, could get some sleep tonight, but it wouldn't be for a while longer.

To his credit, Uncle Glen's only comment after hearing the entire story was, "Next time you'll know enough to call the cops a little sooner."

"Yes, sir," Moses agreed, subdued.

When his police officer relative had finally departed, they sat for a few minutes around the table. Viola looked at her coffee cup. "This was a stupid idea, drinking caffeine at one A.M. Now I'll never get back to sleep."

"And I'll miss the caravan part of the trip in Europe," Rebel mourned. "I was looking forward to that. What am I going to tell my mother? I got mixed up in a mess where I'll have to go to court and testify? She's supposed to be flying out tomorrow, and she'll never go with me in the middle of this kettle of fish. It'll spoil everybody's trip."

She looked hopefully at her grandmother. "I think they have a really early flight. If they are gone before they hear about this, they'll have a while to cool off before I have to see them."

Gram didn't look encouraging at all. "You're saying we won't wake up in time to talk to them before they get on an airplane, and they won't ever discover we held back information they have a right to have?"

Suddenly inspired, Rebel straightened from her slumped position. "I can't talk to Mom; she'll ask all the wrong questions. But, Gram, you're better at evading issues you don't want to talk about than anyone I know. Will *you* call her? Make it sound like I had only minimal involvement, that it was never dangerous or important, but convince her to stay at the music festival and go on with the caravanning afterward. You can do it so much better than I can," she finished optimistically.

Gram gazed at her coolly. "That's the kind of thing my sons used to say when they wanted to con me into doing something they didn't want to do themselves."

"Well, I don't want to do it," Rebel admitted. "I mean, they'll be upset, and what for? It's all over now. There's no sense in anything spoiling their vacation."

Gram drained her cup and rose to put it in the sink. "I'll be glad when they deliver that dishwasher. Do you realize we'll have a batch of dishes to wash first thing in the morning? Darned if I'll stay up any longer to do them now." She turned back to face those still seated at the table. "And I suppose you've figured out what kind of trouble *I'll* be in when your parents get home and discover just how deeply you were involved in this whole thing? I'm not going to lie to them, Amanda Jane Keeling, even if I could, which won't be possible."

"No, no, I don't want you to *lie*, but I remember Dad saying once that you can dance around the truth better than anyone else he knows. Just *evade*, Gram. You know you're an expert at it."

Gram sighed. "We'll see."

"You can tell Mom, truthfully, that I'm really disappointed not to go on the camping trip. Now I may never get to see Europe. They won't be going back *next* summer."

To her surprise, Gram's eyes suddenly twinkled. "Maybe I will. I never got to go caravanning through Europe. Viola, do you think we're too old to go on a major camping trip?"

"Heck, no," Viola stated. "Is that an invitation? I accept. Next summer."

Everybody but me gets to go, Rebel thought, biting her lower lip.

Gram reached out and rested a hand on her shoulder. "Want to go with me, girl?"

"You mean it?" The surge of pleasure was quickly extinguished. "Oh, Mom will never let me go, not after this!"

"She might, if you're exceptionally good for the next year. Stay completely free of trouble?"

For an entire year? That was a tall order. She wasn't sure she could do it, but it would be worth trying.

Viola looked speculatively at her overgrown grandson. "Might even invite Moses along, get him out of his father's hair for a month. Be a relief to both of them. We'd be in one of those motor-home things, right? Room for four people?"

Gram nodded. "Not much privacy. And I'm not sure how comfortable a bed in one of them would be for somebody as tall as he is."

"He's used to curling up," Viola said. "He even slept that way before he got to be over six feet tall."

Rebel's motivation increased incrementally. A month touring fabulous, long-heard-about countries, with Moses along to keep things interesting? "Would you want to come, if we go?" she asked.

"Okay by me," Moses said, grinning. "Anything to ward off my dad trying to make a lawyer out of me." He pushed back his chair. "Since we're both stuck here until the authorities decide what to do with our counterfeiters, maybe you would like to collaborate with me on this script I'm trying to put together. While we're helping Old Vi and your gram fix up this place."

Viola had a sudden thought. "Did any of those people who put down money on rooms really intend to rent them? Or were they all members of that gang? Do we have to start all over again finding renters?"

"I suspect the girl driving the getaway car was the one that looked like a model," Rebel said regretfully. "Uncle Glen said she had long dark hair. That was all he could see of her."

"And that twit with the purple hair was one of them. Cross him off your list of rented rooms," Moses said. "The giggling girls may have been legit."

"I must have missed something," Viola said, rising to contribute her own cup to the collection in the sink. "Why did that fellow snatch his money back from the Dolzyckis and practically run over you? It was counterfeit, wasn't it? He could have just gone home and made another one, so why risk stealing it back and getting his picture taken while he was running away?"

"One of the other ones was renting an apartment in Dad's building," Moses contributed. "I recognized him. He shops at the deli all the time. The guy who bought the candy bar with a bogus bill wasn't supposed to have spent any of it so close to home, I'll bet. After all, if it was discovered when the Dolzyckis took it to the bank, an investigation might well have extended to them just because they live in the same building. That's just a guess, but you see if that doesn't bear out."

Rebel had forgotten how tired she was; she probably had too much adrenaline still in her system to fall asleep immediately anyway. "Are we going to have something exciting in this script? Counterfeiters? Murders? Kidnappers?"

Gram shook her head, speaking to Viola. "Nice ordinary couple of kids we've got here," she said. "I thought they were just making things up this time, and it was real. We're going to have to watch them."

"Always have," Viola said affectionately, resting a hand on Moses' shoulder. "Always will."

Rebel saw that he was looking at her, still faintly smiling.

When he winked at her, she decided then and there that a month's camping trip in Europe would be worth striving for.

Whether or not she could stay out of trouble for that long, and so win her parents confidence, remained to be seen.

But she'd try. She'd sure give it a good try.

She winked back.

Who knew what could happen?